The
Adventures
of
Thunderfoot

Dan Bomkamp

Lovstad Publishing
Poynette, Wisconsin
Lovstadpublishing@live.com

ISBN: 0692489940
ISBN-13: 978-0692489949
(Previous ISBN: 0615750508)

Printed in the United States of America

Cover design by Lovstad Publishing
Cover photo by Dan Bomkamp
On the cover: Alex Cole & Charlie
as Thunderfoot and the dog.

Books by Dan Bomkamp:

The Adventures of Thunderfoot
More Adventures of Thunderfoot
Thanks, Thunderfoot
The Gosey
Big Edna
Voyageur
Lost Flight
Tag
Whiteout
Spirit: the Castle Rock Cougar

Dan Bomkamp

DEDICATION

This book is dedicated to my Dad. He instilled in me at a very early age, a love of the outdoors. Our time together was much too short, but in that time, I learned more from him than many sons learn in a lifetime.

Foreword

I grew up in a beautiful small town situated in the Wisconsin River valley, and I was lucky enough to have a father who took me with him on outdoor adventures as soon as I was out of diapers. I can't actually remember the first time I went, being so young, but my Dad's love of the outdoors certainly rubbed off on me.

Except for my college years, I have lived in the same town and hunted and fished the rivers, lakes, and hills of the area all my life. In fact, my livelihood has been made in the sporting goods industry for many of those years. I've been very lucky to be in a business associated with my love of the outdoors.

But, for many years, I was lacking one thing to complete my outdoor enjoyment, which was a son with whom to share the fun. I had come close to getting married once, but fishing trips and hunting expeditions seemed more important than shopping and domestic stuff, so we parted ways. The years went by and soon I was pretty set in my ways, and still single.

Many of my friends had sons they took along on our trips. I enjoyed the time I spent with them, but I always wished I could share my outdoor experiences with someone of my own.

That wish was fulfilled the day I met Thunderfoot, and since that day we have had so many adventures that I felt I had to share them....thus this book.

Thunderfoot is both a real person and a combination of people. James Buroker is the young man after whom I modeled Thunderfoot. He was my neighbor and best buddy from the time he was about 13 until he graduated from high school and moved on to a job, wife, and family. After James...or "Jamie" as we called him had grown up, I made a decision to host a foreign exchange student. I hosted a boy from Norway, and I had such a good time with him that I have hosted over 30 boys in the last two decades. I now have "sons" all over the world and not a day goes by that one of them or another surprises me with an email, phone call or visit. While they lived with me we did a lot of fishing and hunting and those experiences have given me a wealth of ideas for this book.

Kids impart a special happiness and enthusiasm to everything they do, especially those activities in the outdoors where there are so many variables that can turn a simple outing into a hilarious adventure. They bring a special thrill to a hunt or a fishing trip and make it all fun again for an old-timer. They find a way to make an old guy feel young again.

I've been very lucky to have so many "Thunderfoots". They're all different, but they're all very much the same too. They share the joy of youth and the carefree attitude that more adults should be lucky enough to have. Together we have had great times, and I hope you will enjoy reading about some of them in this book.

~~ Dan Bomkamp ~~

The Adventures of Thunderfoot

Thunderfoot

Sometimes you know right away when you meet a person that you're going to like them. This kid was one of those who I liked as soon as he said hello. He came through the door of my sport shop as I was sitting behind the counter working on some invoices. A younger, smaller version of himself was following along behind him as he smiled and strolled up to the counter.

"Hi," he said, sticking his hand out, "My name is James, and this is my brother Caleb, like in the Bible."

"Hi James," I said, shaking hands with him, and "Hi Caleb." Caleb was a little shy but James wasn't in the least.

"My mom and Caleb and I just moved in over there," he said as he pointed down the street. "So, I guess I'm your new neighbor."

"Well, welcome to the neighborhood, what can I do for you?" I asked.

"Oh nothing. We're just going to look if that's all right."

"No problem, look all you want," I said.

He and Caleb began looking over the rods and reels, and I heard him advise Caleb not to touch stuff as they walked up and down the aisles. He was about 12 or 13, fairly tall, but pretty skinny. He was at that age where he was on the edge of a growth spurt. His hair was light brown and he had the brightest blue eyes I'd ever seen. When he smiled they seemed to sparkle. Caleb was eight or nine and quite a bit shorter, but you could tell right away that they were brothers.

After a while James came over to the counter and dug a quarter out of his pocket for a beef jerky. He tore it in half and shared it with Caleb.

"Well, we better be getting home. Thanks for letting us look around."

"You're welcome any time," I told him, and out the door they went.

The next day I heard someone shouting, "Go Rennie! Go Rennie!" I opened the door and stepped out to see James on a skateboard being pulled down the street by a huge red Doberman. I waved to him and he gave me a wave back as he lurched down the street. I went back inside and soon I heard him yelling, "Stop Rennie Stop!" A minute later he came in through the front door.

"Do you want to meet my dog?" he asked.

I had always had a little hesitancy with Dobermans. "Is he friendly?"

"Oh yeah, he's a real baby...he's not mean at all."

I walked out and met Renegade who was as mild mannered as a kitten.

"He likes to pull me on my skateboard but sometimes I have a hard time to get him to stop," James said.

He was quite a dog. James and I stood and talked a while and he told me that he had just completed the Hunter's Safety class. "I hope I can go hunting sometime," he said. "My grandpa might take me. My dad lives in another town, and I don't think he'll be able to take me."

"You know," I said, "I've got a friend who has lots of squirrels on his farm and he told me I was welcome to hunt there any time I liked. How about you and I go on Saturday?"

James thought that was a great idea, and he went to see if his mom would agree. A short time later he came back with a yes from his mom and a .22 rifle that his grandpa had given him. I outfitted him with an old hunting jacket that didn't fit me any more and some old pants that were in the same situation. We had to roll up the cuffs on the jacket and the pants cuffs but they worked ok. I had a hat that was a little too large but it too would work. Footwear wasn't a problem since his feet were nearly as big as mine. Some of my extra hunting boots worked just fine for him.

When Saturday came, we drove to my friend's farm and parked the truck. Soon we were walking up the ridge road to the top of the hill. We had only gone a few yards when he dislodged a rock that rolled down the hill, clattering all the way. A few yards farther along he tripped and fell down. We didn't go much farther when he stepped on a dead branch that broke and made a loud crack.

I slowed up a little and watched him as he proceeded up the hill ahead of me. He was in a semi-crouch, like he was sneaking up on an enemy bunker. He was watching up the hill and not watching where his feet were going.

"Hey Thunderfoot," I said, "Maybe you should watch where you're putting your feet so you won't chase away all the squirrels."

"Thunderfoot?" he asked with a grin.

"Yeah...you make as much noise as thunder when you walk. Try to sneak and avoid all the things that make noise when you walk."

"Okay," he said grinning widely.

We continued up the hill and suddenly an apparently deaf squirrel came bounding off the bank and onto the road. The squirrel saw us just as Thunderfoot saw it and off they went down over the side of the hill. Thunderfoot was scrambling through the brush as the squirrel shinnied up a tree.

The hillside was nearly vertical, and I'm one of those guys who would rather stay on top of the hill once I've made it to the top, so I wasn't too happy about working my way down to where Thunderfoot was looking up into the treetops.

"I see him," Thunderfoot said.

He aimed his rifle and shot. I saw the squirrel as it hopped over to my side of the tree. I wanted him to shoot it, so I moved and the squirrel hopped back to his side.

Bang! The squirrel came back to my side. I moved again and back it went to his side. *Bang!* Back the squirrel came to my side. I moved again and tried to get back a little farther so I could see him better. Suddenly I slipped and started down the hillside backwards at a very rapid rate stopping only when I ran backwards into an old barbed-wire fence that was hidden in a grove of prickly ash. I hit the fence and went over it backwards. My head and shoulders smacked on the ground and my gun flew from my hands. My legs and feet were hanging on the fence.

The squirrel must have thought there had been an earthquake because he took off through the top of the trees hopping from limb to limb. Thunderfoot took off in hot pursuit shooting every so often and he and the squirrel got farther and farther away. After a while the shooting stopped and everything got very quiet.

I decided I it would be a good idea to get off the fence, but my pants were solidly hooked in the barbs and I couldn't free them. My only option was to take off my pants, so I undid my belt and slid out of them, leaving them on the fence. I was standing there in the middle of the prickly ash grove trying to retrieve my pants when Thunderfoot came huffing and puffing over the top of the hill.

He stopped short when he was me standing there in my underwear. "What'cha doin?" he asked.

"I'm trying to get my pants out of the fence," I said. I finally freed them and put them back on. Then I looked around for my gun and saw it was way down in the middle of the prickly ash so I waded in and got it, tearing many gashes in my hide. I finally hauled y battered body up the hill and onto the road.

"I'm out of bullets," Thunderfoot said. "Jeez, that must hurt."

He was looking at about a dozen punctures in my body. He stepped around behind me and his eyes got wide when he saw the hind end of my pants all ripped out.

"I think I'll live," I said, "but I think I've had enough hunting for today."

He nodded knowingly. "You know," he said, "next time I think I'll bring my .410 shotgun...my rifle doesn't shoot very straight."

We walked down the hill to the truck and when we got there I got out a first aid kit from the glove box and dabbed iodine on my cuts and scrapes. "I hope you're not disappointed that we're quitting," I said. "I'm about finished for the day."

"Oh no, that's ok. I had a lot of fun." He tried to look serious but then he burst out laughing. "That was so cool when you went over the fence...boom!"

His laughter was infectious and soon we both were laughing like crazy, tears running down our faces. "That poor squirrel must have thought it was the end of the world when I crashed through that hillside." We laughed even harder.

Soon we started back to town and Thunderfoot sat quietly in the truck for a while. Then he turned with his big blue eyes sparkling and said, "This was a real good day. I got to go hunting....saw some really funny stuff, and got a new nickname. Thunderfoot. I like it."

It had been a good day, and I had a new hunting buddy.

Thanks, Thunderfoot.

The Great Duck Excursion

We looked like a remnant of the *Lost Battalion* as our convoy of four pickups wound slowly down the sand trail to the site of our hunting camp on the high bank of the duck marsh. In addition to two adults, and two semi-adults, we had five teenagers and five golden retrievers with us on our annual pilgrimage for opening day.

Earlier that morning at 6:15 a.m. Thunderfoot had begun banging on my front door. When I got there he was standing in the middle of a mound of gear that could have sustained an excursion to the North Pole. We had made plans to leave that morning at nine a.m., so I wasn't even close to being ready to go...or to get up from bed yet.

"I thought I should get here a little early so we can load the truck," he said.

"A little early? We're not leaving until nine."

"I didn't want to oversleep so I set my alarm for five a.m.," he said smiling like it was the obvious thing to do under the circumstances.

"Yeah, it's almost 6:30. You better start loading," I said sleepily. I turned to go back to the bedroom to get dressed. "Load my stuff while you're at it," I said, since my gear was already piled on the porch. My three golden retrievers saw the guns and boots and camouflage clothes and went nuts, galloping around the house barking while Thunderfoot encouraged them.

"Yeah, that's it girls. Today is the day!" he said, and the dogs got even more excited.

Obviously my idea of taking a short nap was not going to happen, so I got ready for the day.

A few minutes later I heard the whole gang in the house. I found Thunderfoot in the kitchen looking into the refrigerator. "I thought you were going to load the truck," I said.

"I did...what's for breakfast? I hope the others aren't late."

One of my friends and his two teenaged sons, along with

their golden retriever, Abby, pulled into the driveway a while later at just the appointed time. Then our two semi-adults arrived, they were former teens who hunted with us, but who had now come to the age where we could trust them alone. We could even trust them with the care of a real teenager and his golden retriever Alex.

Abby and Alex were the brother and sister of my youngest golden, Sophie. She was running excitedly back and forth to the truck with her mom Sally, and her grandma, Bea. It was kind of a family thing.

Next, Thunderfoot's two best buddies arrived. They flew in on their bikes, baskets loaded to the brim with gear and food and the group was complete.

We arrived at our campsite a short time later and began unpacking the trucks and setting up our camp. It didn't take long with so many workers. In a short time we had a fire pit dug, four tents pitched, our gear sorted out into the assigned tents, and a famished bunch of kids and dogs waiting for a pre-hunt lunch. Funny, it seemed that I had just fed Thunderfoot an hour or so ago, but he was starving as were the bottomless pits he called friends.

Soon it was an hour until the noon opening time for the season, so everyone began getting into their hunting gear. Camo clothing flew, boots were tugged on, and shells and guns were unpacked and distributed while a frenzied pack of dogs galloped around urging their masters to hurry up. Finally everyone was assigned to his blind and dog, and we took off for the swamp.

Thunderfoot and I took Bea and Sophie with us to a blind on the "Grassy Puddle", while Sally went with another group. The rest split up on other ponds in the marsh. We put our decoys on the water and got our blind in shape, then settled the dogs down while we waited for noon to come.

With fifteen minutes to go, the sky began to fill with ducks spooked by other hunters who were getting into their spots elsewhere in the marsh. "Cool, there's millions of them,"

Thunderfoot said, watching the flocks of birds come and go from every direction.

We waited. Ten minutes to go. Five minutes to go. Two minutes...one minute. The noon siren from town sounded and the season was officially open. One of our other groups fired a couple of shots and as we turned to look we saw a couple of teal coming our way. They were like little gray and blue missiles skimming just above the grass...coming right at us.

"Get ready...here they come," I said. I got my gun ready and when they were in range I said, "Now!" I stood and shot the lead duck. It dropped into the pond and Bea jumped into the water to fetch it. Thunderfoot just stood there looking dumbstruck.

"Why didn't you shoot?" I asked.

"Do they always go that fast? Holy cow...I didn't think they went that fast. I wasn't ready."

"You have to be quick. They aren't just going to flutter around out there and wait for you to shoot them," I said as Bea came into the blind with the teal. I put the duck away and we sat down to wait for another target. In a couple of minutes a lone wood duck started toward our decoys from the other end of the pond.

"Here he comes," I said quietly. "Get ready and take him...I'm not going to shoot."

Thunderfoot got into position, jumped to his feet, and fired one shot at the duck. His shot nailed one of the decoys about three feet behind the wood duck as it passed in front of the blind. The decoy made a large splash as the steel shot hit it, then turned on its side and began sinking in a flurry of bubbles. Bea looked over her shoulder at me and then at Thunderfoot.

"Wow, I got him!"

Thunderfoot was watching the decoy sink but then looked around as the blind began shaking. He looked up at me and saw I was laughing so hard that I was making the entire blind vibrate, so hard that it might fall down.

"Jeez, get a grip...it's not that funny," he said when he realized what he had done.

I finally came back to my senses and while we waited for some more ducks, I reminded him that shooting at a moving bird involved leading it.

We hunted the rest of the day and I got another duck but Thunderfoot failed to connect. We sat in the blind until the time had come for the days shooting to stop and then I went out and picked up the decoys. When I got back to the blind I saw Thunderfoot looking to the west at the reddish glow of the sun as it dropped below the horizon. As we watched, a flock of ducks settled into a pond a short distance away, just as the last rays of daylight disappeared.

"Wow, that was pretty," he said.

"That's what I told you about duck hunting," I said. "Or any hunting for that matter isn't about how many you kill. It's a lot more than that. It's about being in such a beautiful place with people who you enjoy being with. It's about seeing stuff like that sunset."

We hiked up the marsh toward the glow of the campfire. Some of the others were already back and were beginning supper. "I suppose you'll feel the need to tell the others that I shot a decoy," Thunderfoot said.

I grinned at him. "It would be a pretty good story, but I guess it's not necessary. Maybe it will be our little secret."

I could see his smile in the dim light as he put his arm around my neck and gave me a squeeze. "Ok buddy," he said.

"Ok buddy."

Thanks, Thunderfoot.

The Big Gun

There was just enough light from the stars for us to see where we were going. Thunderfoot and I were crunching across the frozen pasture to a goose blind near Horicon Marsh. Our little duck hunting group had arranged to rent some blinds and had left home very early to get to the farm before first light. The farmer was waiting for us when we pulled into his yard. He took us to the edge of the field and pointed us in the general direction of the blinds to which we were assigned.

The blinds were pretty crude, consisting of two sheets of 4' x 8' plywood and two sheets of 4' x 4' plywood joined in the corners by steel fence posts that were driven into the ground. A couple of holes were drilled in the corners of each plywood sheet and strung with wire that held the sheets to the posts. Inside each blind there was a wooden bench and about a thousand empty shotgun shells, a hundred empty pop cans and assorted candy bar wrappers, and other leftovers from previous hunter's lunches.

We had stopped earlier at an enterprising diner in town that catered to the goose hunting crowd by opening at 3 a.m. We filled our sleepy group with pancakes and eggs before we got to the farm, hoping that our teenagers would be able to last until at least noon on the sandwiches and snacks we had brought with us.

I was carrying two guns and the ammo bag, and Thunderfoot was carrying his gun and the lunch. As we crunched along we soon began to pick out the shapes of the blinds. Soon we came to ours which was right along the edge of the field at the fence.

"Is this it?" Thunderfoot asked.

"Yeah...I think so," I said.

"Cool, it's like a little fort."

We unwired the corner of the blind and climbed inside.

After we cleared the middle of the floor of empties and trash we began to unpack our gear. I got my 12-guage pump gun out, loaded it and stood it in the corner against the side of the blind. Then I slid my 10-guage single shot out of the case and loaded it with one of the 3 ½ inch magnum shells. Thunderfoot's mouth dropped open when he saw the gun and the huge shell.

"What's that thing?"

"That's my 10-guage. I thought I'd bring it along in case the geese begin flying too high. It will give us a little more range."

"Can I shoot it?" he asked.

"Well, we'll see. Let's shoot our 12-guages for a while and then maybe later you can try it." I wasn't sure about him shooting the big gun in the first place. For one thing it weighed eleven pounds and was hard to lift and shoot even for a big guy. It also had the kick of an angry mule and I didn't know if his scrawny little shoulder would handle it.

I hoped he'd just let it go and not think about it again.

We got our lunch out and our extra shells and made everything ready for the geese to start flying. Soon we could see the eastern sky begin to turn from black to a dark blue as dawn approached. The blue turned to gray and then things began to have shape. The formerly featureless pasture came into view. We could see the other blinds where our hunting buddies were waiting like we were for the first geese to come from the marsh and begin their trip to the surrounding fields for their breakfast.

The wind was right out of the north and had a distinct bite to it. Fortunately our backs were to the wind but it didn't take long for us to get chilled. We watched and listened and in a short time we could hear the gabbling of the geese as they awoke from their night on the marsh below us. Then the gabbling became honking and the first wave of two or three thousand geese rose into the air like a swirling cloud and began drifting toward the edge of the marsh....coming our way.

Thunderfoot was gripping his gun so hard that his knuckles were white. As the geese began to drift our way his eyes got as big as saucers. "Holy cow, there's a million of them....here they come."

But, instead of coming over us, the geese drifted to our right and a blind with some of our hunting partners began shooting at them. One goose fell from the clouds and the honking became almost deafening. There was more shooting as the geese moved on and then one of Thunderfoot's buddies raced from the blind and proudly retrieved his goose. He held it up to show us and we signaled a thumbs-up to him.

For the next hour geese came constantly from the marsh. Some flocks were just a dozen or so while others held hundreds or maybe a thousand. It was amazing to see so many geese to say the least. Every time some came near, we would shoot. Thunderfoot would spring up and empty his gun every time. He never shot once or twice, but used all three shells every time. We were finishing our third box of shells and still didn't have a goose in the blind.

"Maybe we should try the big gun," he said.

I didn't answer him.

"I bet that big gun would get one."

I pretended that I didn't hear him.

"You know...that big..."

"Ok, I heard you. Go ahead and try it, but remember it'll kick hard so be ready for it."

He had a grin from ear to ear as he hoisted the goose blaster to his shoulder. The gun was about four and a half feet long, almost as tall as he was. He looked like a crazed maniac as he scanned the sky for a victim.

"Be careful with that thing," I said. "It'll kick the snot out of you if you're not careful."

He looked at me with one of those "yeah right" looks.

A minute later a lone goose came from the marsh and was headed right for us. It was real low and honking like mad, as if it had been left behind by the flock. Thunderfoot hunkered down and waited. The goose came closer and closer.

"Get up and get ready to shoot, he's coming," I urged.

Thunderfoot struggled to his feet and raised the goose cannon to his shoulder just as the goose came into range. "Shoot!" I said.

The goose came closer. Thunderfoot raised the gun and followed it with the sight on the end of the barrel. It came closer. He raised the gun following it as it came over us. "Shoot!" I said.

The goose was right overhead when Thunderfoot touched off the shell. The blast made the whole blind shake and it seemed as if every goose in the marsh stopped honking for an instant. It even seemed like the wind stopped blowing. The recoil from the gun was directed right into the top of Thunderfoot's shoulder. He had his right hand tightly wrapped around the stock and his thumb came back and hit him right on the end of the nose causing his eyes to flood with tears. His head snapped back and his cap flew off his head and over the side of the blind. The goose flew on probably vowing never to go so close to one of those little plywood boxes again.

Smoke curled up from the end of the barrel as Thunderfoot lowered the gun and looked at me with a bewildered look in his face. Tears were running down his cheeks and he had a vacant stare in his eyes. "Holy cow...I think I broke my nose."

Well, that did it...I fell back against the side of the blind laughing so hard that I lost my footing in the piles of empty shells and slid right down to the ground. I felt kind of bad about laughing but there was nothing I could do about it. Thunderfoot rubbed his injured nose, wiped his eyes on his sleeve and then began laughing too. "Jeez, you weren't kidding about that thing kicking were you? Where's my hat?"

Remembering his hat popping off his head and flying out of the blind cracked me up again. I couldn't talk, but just pointed over the side until he finally figured out what I was trying to say. He opened the corner of the blind and retrieved his hat.

When he came back into the blind we sat and chuckled for a while about the episode and suddenly he began to grin as he saw

13

his buddy Scott trotting across the pasture toward our blind.

"Here comes Scott. Can I let him shoot the big gun?" he asked with an evil grin on his face.

Thanks, Thunderfoot.

A Memorable Christmas

I was just putting the finishing touches on a big pan of venison stir-fry when Thunderfoot flew through the front door, stomping snow off his boots.

"The snow's a foot deep! *Mmm* that smells good," he said.

He had tried venison for the first time that fall and the stir-fry was his favorite recipe, so I made it for him on the night before Christmas Eve. We both had "family duties" for the next few days and I wanted him to come over for supper. I had a couple of special presents for him.

He heaped his plate with venison and began telling me about all the presents he had at home under the Christmas tree. He had been rattling and worrying them for a week and pretty much had everything figured out as to what it was.

"That's no fun," I said. "I like to be surprised."

"Not me, when I know I've got a prize, I just can't stand it to wait."

"Have you looked under my tree when I haven't been looking?" I asked.

"No, that's your stuff, not mine."

"I wouldn't be so sure. I think there's some stuff there with your name on it."

Well, from then on he couldn't concentrate on his food. He kept looking at the tree and trying to see the tags on the packages.

"If you're done, let's do the dishes and then we can see what's there for you," I said.

He flew to the sink and began washing dishes faster than I could get them from the table. We had the kitchen cleaned up in a matter of minutes. Then we walked over to the tree and I said, "Take a look at that red one there."

When he grabbed the package the paper came off so fast it looked like an explosion. He tore open the box and a pair of camouflage coveralls fell onto the floor.

"Try them on and see if they fit," I said.

He moved the wrapping paper and carefully laid the coveralls on the floor, straightening out the legs and arms. Then he lay down on top of them checking the sleeve length and leg length. He looked up with a huge grin on his face and proclaimed them to be perfect.

"These are great. Now I can get rid of those old green ones," he said.

That was exactly what I had in mind. The old green ones were "park bench" green and were about three sizes too large for him. He swam in them even with the sleeves and legs rolled up. The crotch hung down about ten inches too low and he had to kind of waddle when he walked in them. These new ones would be a lot better for him.

"There's something else for you behind the tree," I said.

He jumped up and dashed to the tree. He stopped in his tracks when he saw a long thin package with his name on it. He reached back and tried to lift it with one hand but couldn't.....it was too heavy. So he took hold of it with both hands and then looked at me in disbelief. He tore the paper off, stopped and looked at me. When he saw the printing on the box he ripped it open and his eyes just about popped out. "Are you kidding me? No way. Holy cow. *No way!* I can't believe it!"

It seemed that full sentences weren't possible just now as he lifted his very own 10-guage shotgun from the box. He pulled it to his shoulder a couple of times and aimed it at imaginary geese that were flying through the living room. Then he stopped and looked at me. "Is it really mine?"

"Your name was on the box," I said grinning.

He laid the gun down like it was the crown jewels and then came over and put his arms around me and gave me a back-popping hug. "Thanks a million," he said.

I had a pretty big lump in my throat and my eyes were full of tears as I hugged him back.

"That's the best Christmas present I ever got," he said. "But I feel bad, I don't have anything for you."

"I've got everything I need," I told him. "You've given me more fun and laughter in the past few months than I ever could have imagined possible. You couldn't give me anything better than all of those great memories."

He took a deep breath and nodded. He put his new coveralls on and then his boots and picked up his new shotgun. "I'll leave my jacket and the box for the gun here if it's ok," he said. I said it was fine and that he could pick them up after Christmas.

He gave me another big hug and stepped out into the night. I watched out the window as he crossed my snowy back yard. He would walk a few feet, stop and sight down the barrel of the gun at some imaginary goose, then hike a way farther and repeat his little imaginary hunt. When he got to the edge of the yard he stopped under the streetlight, waved and disappeared into the darkness at the edge of the light.

It was one of those moments that you save for a long, long time.

Thanks, Thunderfoot...Merry Christmas.

Ice Boating

I was snuggled in my recliner with my comforter over my lap contemplating a nap. Outside the wind was howling across the glistening snow and making little whirlwind-like swirls. I happened to look out the window across the back yard and saw a mound of clothes wading through the snow carrying an ice fishing bucket. A minute later the clothes mound flew in through the front door, letting in a blast of cold air. The clothes mound stomped its feet and soon a pile of mittens, scarves, caps, coats and sweaters began growing on my living room floor. As the pile of clothes got larger Thunderfoot emerged grinning like a mad musher from the Yukon.

"I can't believe you're not ready yet," he said.

"I am ready...ready for a nap."

"No way, we're going ice fishing. The other day you said we'd go ice fishing on Saturday and this is Saturday."

"I didn't know it would be -20 on Saturday when I said that. It's like a blizzard outside. We can't fish in that kind of wind."

"Oh piffle, it's nice out...almost balmy."

"Balmy my butt," I said.

He gave me one of those 'I can't believe that would stop you' looks. "If you dress right it's not bad at all." Then he looked at me with those sad eyes he was so good with and I shook my head.

"Once we get the shanty set up and the stove lit we'll be inside and it won't matter how cold it is," he said nodding his head up and down.

I knew it was hopeless to argue with him so I got dressed and a half hour later we were plowing through the snow drifts on the sand road that led to the lake. We pulled into an empty parking lot. Of course no one else was crazy enough to be out there like we were, so it was no surprise we were alone at the lake. We unloaded the gear from the back of the pickup and piled all of the gear onto the shanty which had a plastic sled on the bottom. Thunderfoot happily grabbed the rope from the sled and pulled it toward the bank that led down to the lake. When he got on the ice his feet kept walking but the heavy sled didn't move and soon he was marching in place. He gave me a sorrowful look and handed me the rope. "We need someone who is...um, heavier to pull. I'll run ahead and drill the holes."

I had a pair of ice cleats with me so I sat down and attached them to my boots and then started pulling the sled down the lake right into the teeth of the wind. Several minutes later I caught up to Thunderfoot at the other end. He had the auger with him and had begun to try to drill a hole. Of course with no snow on the ice, once the auger bit into the surface, Thunderfoot began spinning around as he turned the handle. He was too light to put enough pressure on the auger to make a hole. He gave me another of those sorrowful looks and handed me the auger. "I'll scoop the ice chips out after you drill."

I drilled four holes and he did manage to clean the ice chips out. We tried to light the stove but the wind was blowing so hard that it was impossible. "We'll have to light it inside when we get the shanty up," I shouted over the wind.

The shanty was attached to the sled and just unfolded when it was set up, so we unloaded all of the buckets and other gear from on top of it and positioned it over the four holes. On one end there was a zippered door. Thunderfoot lifted up the end and unzipped the door so he could arrange the aluminum frame inside. When the door was opened we heard a *Whump!* when the wind opened the tent up like a hot air balloon. It immediately began sliding over the ice with us handing on like rag dolls. I was on my knees and it only took a short way for me to fall over on my back. Thunderfoot's feet flew out from under him and he landed on his belly. Both of us were being dragged over the ice and we began going faster and faster.

Since I was wearing ice cleats on my boots, I tried to put one foot down on the ice to slow us down. As soon as the ice cleat hit the ice it came off my boot and launched into the air like a Ninja throwing star and disappeared in a shower of ice chips. By now we were going at Warp 3 so I carefully put the other boot down and applied pressure on the ice more carefully. The cleat began throwing up a rooster tail of ice chips and making a screeching sound as it was drug across the ice. But, we began slowing down and soon our rooster tail began to disappear.

We finally came to a complete stop in the cattails at the other end of the lake, where he had come from in the first place. We were both laughing like crazy. I looked over at Thunderfoot. His face was covered with ice chips and snow. Snot was running down from his nose to his chin. "Pull the tent down!"

"I can't...my nose is running," he said.

That cracked us up again and be both laughed crazily. Finally he wiped his nose on the back of his mitten and got to his knees and pulled the nylon shanty down onto the sled. The shanty deflated and I was able to release my death grip on the sled. I sat up and looked back down the lake. Our gear was strung all over creation and as I got my breath one of my poles came sliding along right to me. A little while later my cap slid up too. "I think we better retrieve our stuff and give up!" I shouted over the whine of the wind. Thunderfoot nodded in agreement.

We worked our way back upwind and gathered our gear. I found my other cleat after a long search and we headed back to the truck and loaded up. As we closed the doors and started the truck Thunderfoot looked out over the frozen lake. "I bet they would have bit today too," he said shaking his head. "But all that noise you made scraping that cleat probably spooked all the fish anyway." He looked over at me with an impish grin.

Half an hour later we were home, all the gear stowed away. I hung up our clothes to dry. I heard the refrigerator door open. Thunderfoot was looked around inside the fridge and then over at me. "Boy, fishing sure makes me hungry."

"Breathing makes you hungry."

Big grin.

Thanks, Thunderfoot.

The Great Bunny Hunt

I was backing my way through a nearly solid wall of berry briars when the sound of a shot from Thunderfoot's 20-guage came from the other side of the tangle. A couple of seconds later I heard another shot, followed by yet another. I waited for a short time and then resumed my backward bulldozing until I got to the other side.

Thunderfoot was nowhere to be seen, but he soon came stomping back over a little rise, stuffing shells into his gun. I raised my eyebrows as if to ask where the rabbit was only to be met with a "don't even ask" look.

"Well?"

"I can't believe I missed him," he said. "I had him right in my sights."

"Did you lead him?"

"No...should I have?" he asked with a puzzled look.

"Yeah...remember the ducks? Rabbits are the same. They're moving not sitting still."

Somehow he had figured that if he was shooting a shotgun he was shooting a bullet that was about three feet across because of the way the pellets spread out when they left the gun. He got an enlightened look on his face as I mentioned the ducks. We started off through the woods to the next tangle of briars.

Again, he snuck around to the far side of the berry patch and I, ever the faithful dog, plowed into the mess with the hope of driving a rabbit out in front of him. I had only gone a short way when the briars got so thick that I had to get down and crawl. I hadn't gone far when another barrage of shooting started on the other side. This time there were three fast shots followed by one lone shot long after the others.

I went a few feet farther and the shooting started again. This time he shot only three times. As I emerged from the thicket, bleeding profusely from a gash delivered to my left ear

21

by a particularly nasty berry bush, I expected to find him with a limit of rabbits.

His hat was on sideways and he was looking pretty peeved. "I did just what you said and they still all got away."

"How far did you lead them?"

"I don't know...maybe ten feet."

"Ten feet!"

We walked over to the spot where he had shot at the second rabbit. There in the snow were rabbit tracks going up to a bare spot where his shot had hit the ground. Then the rabbit tracks made a right angle turn and went off into the distance. The bunny had taken a turn to the right when Thunderfoot blew up the snow in front of him.

"You shot a bit too far ahead," I said. "But I bet you gave him a thrill when he saw the snow blow up."

Thunderfoot reloaded and we started toward the best spot in the woods. This was the honey hole, the *Valhalla of all Rabbitdom*, the downtown gathering spot for all the rabbits in the woods.

Many years earlier the woods had been logged. After all the timber was hauled away the loggers bulldozed the limbs and branches into a big ditch, making a *Rabbit Super 8*. There were rabbit trails leading into and out of the place from all over the woods. The only problem was that the rabbits were perfectly safe unless you had a dog that could get into the tangled branches and root them out. Our dog was me. My golden retrievers were duck dogs and turned their noses up at the thought of looking for a lowly rabbit, so I got the job. The trouble was that I was way too big to crawl into the rabbit trails that led into the woodpile.

"How do we get them out?" Thunderfoot asked as we approached the *Bunny Hilton*.

"You get up on that high spot over there," I said pointing to a rise. "I'll climb up there on top of the pile and stomp. If I make enough noise maybe some of the rabbits will run out, and you can shoot them."

"Sounds like a plan," he said as he started walking toward the high spot.

I lay my shotgun on a stump, not wanting to climb through the mess carrying a gun. Then I began working my way up onto the pile of limbs and branches. I had only gone a few feet when a bunny darted out right at Thunderfoot. It nearly went right over his feet and he just stood there and watched it.

"Nice shot," I said chuckling.

He stood there with a mystified look on his face. "I wasn't ready," he said.

I climbed up farther on the pile and started jumping up and down. Rabbits popped out as if someone had yelled fire in a theater. Thunderfoot pulled up on a bunny, and then swung his gun toward another without firing at either one of them. There were rabbits running everywhere, and he was beginning to panic trying to decide which one to shoot at.

I was getting close to the middle of the pile when I stopped to catch my breath. I put one foot down on a branch and felt the pile below me settle. I carefully moved my foot to a larger branch and shifted my weight to that one. A second later the branch broke and the whole section I was standing on collapsed sending me to the basement of rabbit haven. On the way down through the branches, my jacket caught on a branch. It was pulled over my head, like skinning a bunny, and my arms were pinned upward along the side of my head. The only thing I could see was the buttons on my jacket in front of me and the sky above. My feet were hanging in mid-air as I hadn't gone all the way to the bottom of the pile. Hmm, this was not good.

I hung there for a minute trying to figure out how to get out of the mess. Suddenly I could hear a muffled choking sound. It was something like...*hrmf...hrmf.* I wasn't sure what it was, but it was getting closer. Maybe it was a rabid rabbit.

I could feel the pile of wood moving and soon I heard, "Are you ok?" It was Thunderfoot sobbing between fits of laughter. I looked up through the top of the jacket, which was actually the bottom of the jacket and there stood Thunderfoot peering down at me, tears running down his face.

"I think I'm ok as long as the rabbits don't attack me for wrecking their home," I said laughing.

He began clearing away the brush to get me out and after a bit I managed to get on top of the pile. I pulled my jacket down so I could see again. "Did you get any rabbits after all this work?"

"No...I was laughing so hard I couldn't shoot. It was like one of those magic shows...one second you were there and then poof...you were gone."

I started laughing again and we climbed down from the pile.

"Let's go home," he said. "I can't take any more of this and besides...I'm out of bullets."

That's fine with me." This old dog was ready for a nap.

Thanks, Thunderfoot.

Don't Cry Wolf

"We'll put out four tip-ups and then we can each jig with one pole," I said as Thunderfoot and I walked down over the bank and onto the ice of a frozen backwater slough. "You pick the spots for the tip-ups and drill the holes. I'll set up the tip-ups and bait them."

He took off down the ice and carefully selected the best spots for out tip-ups. I followed along behind carrying a bucket with the tip-ups in it and a bait bucket with shiners. We worked for almost half an hour before we got all the tip-ups baited and then drilled two holes for our jig poles, sat down and began fishing.

"Who gets to pull up which tip-up?" Thunderfoot asked.

"You can take them all," I said. "I want to get a good picture of a big northern coming up from the hole for a story I'm going to write, so I'll man the camera." That seemed fine with him, so we worked our jigs and kept an eye on the tip-ups. Suddenly the stillness of the day was interrupted by Thunderfoot. "FLAG!" The cry echoed down the ice as he raced toward one of the tip-ups. This was his first time pulling in a fish on a tip-up, so he was pretty excited.

"Should I pull now?" he asked.

"No....wait until the line spools stops turning. Then when the fish starts to move again, give it a good hard pull."

He carefully lifted the tip-up out of the hole in the ice, eyes glued to the nylon line which was slowly being pulled from the reel. Then it stopped. "He's turning the minnow now to swallow it," I said. "Get ready."

The spool of line began to move again and Thunderfoot jerked on the line and fell over backwards. He clambered to his feet and pulled furiously on the line.

"Take it easy," I warned. "Don't pull it out of his mouth."

He kept pressure on the line and soon a small northern

popped up in the hole and he lifted it out. "Wow, that's fun."

It was his first tip-up fish. We took a quick picture and slid the fish back down the hole. Then we re-set the tip-up and walked back to our jig poles and sat down to fish some more. We had just begun when another flag popped up.

"FLAAAAG!" Thunderfoot was a blur as he took off for the tip-up. I grabbed the camera and headed down the ice. He was waiting for the appropriate time to set the hook, so I lay down on the ice so I could get a picture just as the fish cleared the hole. "Is it a big one?" I asked.

"It feels huge."

I got ready with the camera and Thunderfoot said, "Here he comes." I snapped a picture as a little "snake" northern popped out of the hole.

"I thought you said it was huge."

"Well I thought it was," he said grinning from ear to ear.

We reset the tip-up and started back to our jig poles when another flag popped up. The now familiar cry of "FLAAAAG!" echoed down the lake as Thunderfoot raced toward the fluttering orange piece of vinyl. I got there just as he set the hook. He started pulling in the line but his hands kept jerking back toward the hole, causing him to lose line for a bit, only to gain it back. "Give me time to get the camera ready," I said lying on the ice. He fought the fish back and forth bravely. Soon he said, "Get ready...he's coming up."

The camera clicked perfectly as the water in the hole began to splash and another little "snake" northern popped up. Thunderfoot fell over backwards laughing.

"You little snot!" I said starting back toward the jig poles. Thunderfoot could bait his own tip-ups.

A bit later he plopped down on his bucket. He was quiet. "Uhmmm... I said...Uhmmm."

I looked over at his big grin.

"Sorry" he said.

"Yeah I can tell. You're going to cry wolf one time to often and then we'll miss a picture of a big one because I won't trust you anymore."

"Cry wolf? I'm gonna cry NORTHERN!"

That made me laugh and just then we both noticed the farthest flag had popped up. "FLAAAAG!" He was off to the races.

I didn't feel like running all the way down the lake again so I hollered at him, "Reset the flag when you get done."

He pulled the line and soon I could see him fighting a fish. He yelled, "It's huge....I'm serious!"

I could see his arms jerking back and forth at the hole but I wasn't going to fall for that old trick again. I ignored him.

"This one is huge," he called. "Come and help me... Please, please, no wolf, no wolf."

I gave up and walked down the ice and got to the hole. I had just gotten my camera to my eye when a huge ten pound northern emerged halfway up through the hole. I snapped the picture as the fish twisted to the side....just the picture I was looking for. Thunderfoot slid the fish out onto the ice and then pushed it farther away from the hole.

"Holy cow, you weren't kidding," I said.

"Jeez I thought you'd never come," he said panting.

We unhooked the beautiful fish and took a couple more pictures of Thunderfoot grinning and holding the trophy. Then we slid her back into the water.

"That was very cool," he said. "I like this tip-up fish.... FLAAAAG!"

Thanks Thunderfoot.

Just One Last Time

"They're getting big bluegills at Postel's," Thunderfoot said as he burst through my front door. "They're congregated up where the creek runs into the lake. There're millions of them!"

We had been experiencing a warm spell and the ice was getting much too thin for my tastes and body size. "How are they getting out there?" I asked. "They must be taking boats. The ice is nearly all gone...there can't be any safe way to get to the lake by now."

Postel's "lake" as it was called, was a slough about one quarter of a mile from solid ground in the Wisconsin river bottoms. It could be reached during the dead of winter because the swamp between it and the high bank was frozen. At this time of year, the swamp became impassable. There was no other way to get to the lake.

"The path is ok...they're going out there right now. We can get there too...I'm sure of it. Just wait here, I'll be right back." Thunderfoot took off for his house across the back yard. A few minutes later he came back lugging a 5 gallon bucket that was almost full of huge bluegills. "These came from Postel's this morning," he said.

I looked at the fish and had to admit they were really nice bluegills. "Who caught those?" I asked.

"My neighbor...he went this morning and got them in about two hours. Let's go!"

Thunderfoot's neighbor was a little old guy who didn't weigh much over a hundred pounds dripping wet. Of course neither did Thunderfoot, so he had no worries. But, I was a bit more "full figured" and as agile as a cow, so I had second thoughts about trying to get to the lake. But I had an idea. "Go out in the shed and get my hip boots," I told Thunderfoot.

He stood there with a puzzled look on his face the then his

28

eyes brightened when he realized what I had in mind. He got my boots and in a few minutes we had our ice fishing gear loaded in the pickup and were heading to Postel's.

Thunderfoot led the way down the path to the lake. As we came to the trail that ran out across the swamp he began walking but suddenly his foot went through the frozen muck. He jumped off to the side to keep dry. I carefully stepped into the hole he had made in the ice with my hip boot and then stepped up on solid ice on the other side, quite proud of myself. We went a short way and the same thing happened again. Now I was feeling pretty clever. When we were only a few feet from the edge of the lake and good ice, we had one little area of "swamp ice" left to cover. Thunderfoot zipped right across and I took a deep breath and managed to get across too.

"See, I told you we could get out here," he said as he began drilling a hole.

He was right, the fish were there. And...they were hungry. The sun came out through the clouds and the temperature soared to almost sixty. We fished and had a glorious time sitting in our shirt sleeves, enjoying the spring weather and catching bunches of bluegill.

By mid-afternoon we both had our buckets nearly full. "We better see how many we have," I said. "We must be close to our limits." We both counted our fish and I was one short of my limit while Thunderfoot still needed three. A few minutes later we had all we could legally keep.

"Wow, I don't think I ever had such a good day of fishing," Thunderfoot said. "What a way to end the season."

We packed up and he trotted across that first area of bad ice. He was almost all the way across when he broke through. One of his feet got a little wet but he was quick and agile enough that he scampered off the ice with little trouble.

"You better go around," he said. "It's pretty thin."

"I'll be ok. I've got my hip boots on," I said. I started across the ice. I took two steps and then my left foot broke through.

29

The water was only knee deep, so I was still ok....until I tried to step up onto the ice with my right foot. I lost my balance and went head first into the ice-cold water and mud. I came up from the mire like a whale breaching from the depths and then floundered around in the mud pit for several minutes trying to get out.

Thunderfoot stood there on solid ground and tried to look concerned for my safety, but he was having a hard time keeping a straight face. I finally got to solid ground and started picking up my gear which had been strewn all over the place with my thrashing around. I found all my stuff and then we started down the trail toward the high bank. I slogged along, my boots full of water making a sloshing sound as I walked. My clothes were saturated with an aromatic swamp scent and my mood was much less cheery than it had been earlier.

After a while Thunderfoot got far enough ahead of me that he felt safe. He looked over his shoulder and said, "You know...those hip boots proved to be a pretty good idea." I could tell he was grinning even though he kept his face straight ahead. Wise guy.

Thanks, Thunderfoot.

The Big Mushroom

Thunderfoot and I had parked alongside a gravel road in the hills near town. We were trekking through a pasture toward the hillside on our first mushroom hunt. This was Thunderfoot's first time looking for morels and he was chomping at the bit to get started.

"They look like corncobs with the corn all gone," I said as we walked toward an old dead elm that I had spotted from the road. The tree looked like a prime mushroom tree. "Once you see one you'll know what to look for and won't have any trouble find more."

At the tree I could see several morels sticking up amid the leaves and clutter on the ground. Thunderfoot stopped and began looking around about two feet from one. He was looking everyplace but at the mushroom.

"Look closer to you," I said.

He looked down and spotted the morel. Stooping down to pick it he said, "Cool...there's another over there and jeez....there's another one!" He scurried around picking the mushrooms as if they were going to grow legs and run away from him.

I bent to pick one that was poking up from some dead leaves when I saw movement in the grass as a small snake slithered away. "Jeez!" I said hot-footing it down the slope.

"What was that? Was it a snake? What's going on....are you afraid of snakes?" The little snot was having a ball teasing me.

"No it just startled me," I lied. Actually I am deathly afraid of snakes. You'd think that after spending most of my youth digging around in the river bottoms I'd be used to snakes but they just creep me out. It's so bad that when one of those guys on the animal shows on TV finds a snake, I turn to another program. They just HAVE to pick the dang things up don't they? I won't even touch the page in a magazine with a picture of a snake. I don't understand it but that's the way it is...I don't like snakes.

"Are you really afraid of snakes? You know...I bet there's some rattlers around here. What do you think?" The little monster's eyes were just twinkling.

I ignored him and picked up a substantial stick about five feet long and tested its strength. He looked at me questioningly and I explained to him that this was my mushroom stick. It was used for moving leaves and brush aside when looking for mushrooms and could also be used to beat to death, any smart guy who had snake ideas.

Thunderfoot was hurt to the core to think that I might even suspect him of such notions. We decided that he'd head up the right side of the hill while I'd take the left side. We agreed to meet back at the truck in an hour or so and off we went.

I began looking at dead elms on the lower part of the hill and found several with mushrooms growing around them. In a short time I had a pretty good sack full so I decided to go back to the truck and wait for him.

I laid the tailgate down and sat up on it and soon decided to lay back and closed my eyes. I was sprawled out in the back of the pickup when movement awakened me. Thunderfoot had hopped up and was sitting on the tailgate swinging his legs over the end.

"Ah, sleeping beauty awakes," he said grinning.

"Wow, the sun was so warm and nice that I guess I dozed off. How did you do?"

"Oh not bad," he said. "How about you, did you find any?"

"I've got half a sack or so," I said.

He stood up proudly and opened his sack. It was full to the brim with nice morels. "What do you think of these babies?" he said.

I was impressed, he'd done well.

"I've got one that is so big I had to put it in my spare sack so it wouldn't crush the rest of them," he said. He picked up the second sack and opened it, turning it upside down on the ground at my feet. "Look at this baby."

A three foot blacksnake dropped almost on my feet and I jumped up and let out a shriek that probably sounded like a soprano hitting the high note in an Italian opera. I jumped about three feet in the air while automatically raising my mushroom stick to "kill mode". The snake slithered off into the grass at the roadside while Thunderfoot was staggering around doubled over with laughter. When he saw the look on my face he took off up the gravel road on a dead run with me right behind him, my mushroom stick held over my head like a war club. He was laughing so hard that I nearly caught him but it didn't take me long to figure out that running down the road was not the best thing for an old guy to do, so I stopped and tried to catch my breath.

Thunderfoot stopped a few feet away, just out of mushroom stick range and laughed with delight. "Not afraid of snakes?" He grabbed his belly and laughed so hard he nearly fell down. I finally got my breathing back to normal but my heart beat and blood pressure was probably still about as high as it could go without having "the big one."

"Come on...let's go home," I said turning toward the truck.

"No way....you're gonna hit me with that stick!" he said keeping his distance.

"I won't hit you...you know that."

"Yeah? Well prove it...lose the stick."

He knew he probably wasn't in any danger, but just in case he wanted my stick gone before he got in range. "You know, you shouldn't do something like that to an old man," I said. "What would you have done if I'd have had a heart attack?"

"I guess I'd have had to learn to drive the truck.....uh, the stick?"

I tossed the stick in the ditch and he walked up to me. "Jeez, I never saw you move so fast before or jump so high. I didn't know you could run either." He was grinning from ear to ear.

I raised my hand as if to swat him but grinned. We walked

back to the truck and I carefully avoided the tall grass where the snake had gone, though I doubted he was still around after my little demonstration. We got into the truck and I pulled out onto the gravel and started for home.

Thunderfoot put his hand on my shoulder. "I am sorry...I guess I didn't think you'd be so scared. Jeez, I wouldn't want you to have a heart attack. Who would I have to pick on then?" He grinned at me and winked.

Who indeed?

Thanks, Thunderfoot.

The First Turkey Hunt

Thunderfoot was not a morning person. He was real dependable about being on time for fishing or hunting, as long as the day started at mid-morning or early afternoon. On those occasions he was usually ready to go ahead of time. But early morning trips were not his cup of tea.

I had been forced several times to go to his house and tap on his bedroom window to get him up and hated to do that. I usually ended up waking up the whole household, so the night before the first turkey hunt I suggested that he sleep in my spare bedroom. It would be easier on me and his family if he was where I could wake him up on time. By now he had left wet and muddy clothes and other gear at my house many times, so "his" room was pretty well stocked.

I turned my alarm clock off at 4 a.m. and walked down the hall to his room. I rustled him awake and then went off to dress and to get some toast and cereal ready for breakfast. He didn't seem to be making much noise so I stuck my head into his room. He was sitting on the edge of the bed scratching his head and yawning.

"Get dressed...we've got to get going," I said.

"What?"

"Get up and get dressed. We've got to get to the woods."

He started mumbling about how it was the middle of the night but he did manage to get dressed. I loaded the truck with the decoys and some camouflage netting, while he went to the bathroom. When he finally came out I was all ready to go. He grabbed a piece of toast and we headed out the door. "Jeez, it's the middle of the night," he complained.

"Just wait until you hear that first gobble. Then you'll think this is worth it," I said.

I got no answer. I turned and he was slumped down in the seat with his eyes closed.

35

It was only a fifteen minute drive to the farm where we were hunting so his nap didn't last long enough to suit him. He began grumbling again when I woke him and continued as we started up the ridge road to the top of the hill.

"Shhh.....the turkeys roost just up the hill from here," I said. "We have to walk right below them to get to the top of the hill, so be quiet."

He was awake by now and began stepping as quietly as could, avoiding at least some of the sticks and rocks. We stopped when we got to the top of the hill. "Can you see how this field lays?" I whispered to him.

He nodded.

"The turkeys usually roost over there, I said pointing to the woods. When it gets light they'll fly down to the field and come through the gate into the pastures. The hens usually roost out on the other hill and come into this field when the sun comes up to get warmed up. I'll put the decoys out by the gate and hopefully one of the toms will come to us before he goes to the real hens."

"Sounds like a plan to me," he said grinning in the moonlight.

We unpacked the decoys and slid them onto their metal stakes. Then I stuck them into the ground about fifteen yards from two huge maples that stood as the fence-line below us. We walked over to the maples and cleared the twigs and leaves from the area and hung out camouflage material from some bushes, forming a makeshift blind. We sat down behind the blind to wait, one of us leaning back against each of the maples.

Thunderfoot was wide awake now and it didn't take long for him to get impatient. Every time there was some sound, he'd wiggle around to look where it came from.

"Sit still," I said to him.

"What?"

"Get comfortable and then sit still. You don't dare move or the turkeys will see you. They've got really good eyesight."

"Do they have flashlights?" I could see him grinning in the dim light.

The blackness was turning into a deep purple as an owl hooted from somewhere down the ridge. The sound of the hoot hadn't even faded when a turkey gobbled from his roost. He was just where I had told Thunderfoot he would be.

Thunderfoot sat upright and listened as another turkey answered the first one and then another sounded off.

"They're right where you said they'd be," he said looking surprised.

"Did you doubt the expert?"

He grinned and shook his head. In the next few minutes the woods came alive with the sounds of morning. Now there were at least a dozen turkeys gobbling up and down the ridge. There were a couple of owls hooting and dozens of songbirds chirping. Soon a group of crows began cawing for good measure and a pair of wood ducks whistled as they flew overhead. Thunderfoot was alert now, his big ten-gauge at the ready.

I slipped my favorite diaphragm call into my mouth and gave a couple of quiet yelps, which were immediately answered by at least three toms off to our right. I waited a few minutes and then made the hen yelps again. The toms answered right away but this time they were in a different place. "They're down from the tree," I whispered.

Thunderfoot nodded his head slowly to let me know he understood.

For the next hour or so I called and the toms answered, always moving our way but taking their time and not showing themselves to us. Finally they stopped answering my calls and things became quiet.

"Did they leave?" he asked.

"Some real hens probably came to them. We'll wait and see if they remember us after the real hens go to lay their egg for the day."

Another half hour passed and the toms were quiet. I called every ten minutes or so, but there was no response. Suddenly I heard a humming noise that was new to the woods. I tried to see an insect or bird that might be making the sound but there was nothing that I could see that made it. Then the noise turned from a humming noise into a fairly loud snore. I turned my head and looked over at the now-sleeping Thunderfoot. The warm morning sun was filtering down through the leaves and had taken its toll on my tired partner. I was having a hard time staying awake myself, but I kept calling for another half hour and let him have a little nap.

We had gotten permission for Thunderfoot to be a little late for school but we'd have to get going pretty soon, so I picked up a small stick and poked him a coupe of times.

He blinked his eyes and looked around, not knowing just where he was. Finally he looked at me and smiled.

"Have a nice nap?" I whispered.

"Yup....where are the turkeys?"

"You scared them away with your snoring."

"Bull...I don't snore."

"Ok but we had better be going, you have to go to school you know."

He grimaced but we gathered up our gear and started down the hill. We stopped and looked up the hill at the woods where the turkeys had been when the gobbled.

"You know, if we set up over there by the corner of that fence I think we'd have a better chance tomorrow. That is, if you can get up again."

"Just try to keep me home," he said. "But I'm going to bed a lot earlier tonight."

The next morning things went smoother as far as getting up and getting ready were concerned. Thunderfoot was a bit chattier as we drove through the dark to the farm.

We snuck up the hill and went to the left at the top and then snuck dangerously close to the place where the birds were probably roosting. When we got to the corner or the fence I put the decoys out below us. We hung the netting over some tall weeds and brush and used the corner of the fence for our backrest.

"This is a better place," Thunderfoot whispered. "Now we got them."

But the second morning was a repeat of the first, because the turkeys had roosted in a different place. Instead of being to our right, they were up the hill to the left and we were sitting with our backs to them.

"We can't move now," I whispered. "If they see the decoys they'll come right past us on the right. So, just sit real still and wait."

He nodded that he understood and we waited.

A little while later we heard a faint gobble. I couldn't quite make out where it had come from. "Did you hear that?" I whispered.

"They're right behind us," he whispered back.

"Can you see them?" I asked not daring to turn my head.

"Yup...they're right up in the corner and they're coming our way."

Things just might work out after all. The only problem was that the turkeys were to Thunderfoot's right and it would be hard to move to get the gun into position to shoot at them.

"Move really slowly," I said. "Try to turn as much to your right as you can without them seeing you...real slow."

He scooted his bottom around as much as he dared but he still wasn't in a good position to shoot.

"I can't move any farther without them seeing me," he whispered.

"Just get your gun up slowly to your shoulder. We'll have to wait for them to move far enough to the left for you to get a shot." I slid very slowly to the right so I could see what was going on. Two big toms were heading right for us. They didn't seem to have any idea that there was a little guy with a real big gun waiting for them.

The toms strutted for the decoys and then walked toward them a little ways and strutted again. At the rate they were coming, it would take at least five minutes for them to move far enough for Thunderfoot to get his sights on them.

"No hurry," I said. "We'll just wait for them to get here."

He nodded slightly.

The minutes seemed like hours, but the toms were finally getting close to the point where they had to be so Thunderfoot could shoot. They had about ten feet more to go when one of them stopped and raised his head as if listening to something. Then the other one raised his head too. I stopped breathing thinking they could hear me but I instantly heard the noise the turkeys were hearing.

Across the valley, the farmer was having a ridge logged off and the logger was coming down the ridge road dragging a bunch of logs behind a skidder. It was at least a quarter of a mile away, but the turkeys stopped dead in their tracks. The logger dragged the logs down to a level pasture and got off the skidder to unhook them. Our turkeys turned around and trotted back up the hill into the woods.

Thunderfoot's shoulders sagged as he lowered the gun and turned to me. "What are the odds that he'd come down there with those logs just now?

I just shook my head.

We sat a few minutes longer and then started to get our stuff together. "Well, they never said it'd be easy," I commented. "That's why only one in four hunters gets a turkey."

"That's why they call it turkey hunting instead of turkey shooting," he said grinning. "Oh well, there's always tomorrow."

That's my little trouper.

Thanks, Thunderfoot.

Saying Goodbye to Sally

Thunderfoot was walking across the back yard, but he wasn't in his usual hurry. His head was low and he seemed not to want to get to my house. I had called him earlier and asked him to come over and he knew why. He wasn't in any hurry to confront what waited for him.

He and Sally had been good buddies from the time he started hanging out with me. My older golden retriever Bea, had died shortly after I met Thunderfoot so he had not gotten to know her so well, but Sally was one of his best friends. My third golden Sophie was Sally's daughter and she was also his buddy, but he and Sal had been special friends.

Sally had been sick for quite a while. She had come down with some tumors that the Vet had removed some time ago. For a while after the surgery Sal seemed like a new dog but then we could tell that things were not right with her. Another trip to the Vet the day before had confirmed my fears.

Thunderfoot came into the living room and looked at me questioningly. "I called Dr. Pat," I said. "She's coming down later this morning for Sal."

He looked thunderstruck. "You mean today?" he said.

I nodded. "We can't wait any longer. There isn't anything more they can do for her, and I don't want to see her suffer. We can't keep her going just to make us feel better. She's not going to get better and that's it."

Thunderfoot's eyes welled up with tears and he turned and went into the spare bedroom where Sally was sleeping on her blanket on the floor. I left them alone for a while and then went to the room. Thunderfoot was sitting next to his old friend petting her on the head and talking to her. Sally's tail was wagging as they shared a last minute together.

"I'll drive you to school," I said. "We better get going or you'll be late."

He nodded and then buried his face in Sally's fur. A minute

41

later he came out of the bedroom with red eyes and we drove in silence to the school.

I went home and helped Sally get up. We slowly walked to the door and then out into the yard. We walked and she looked over her domain one last time...her yard, the piece of ground she had guarded and protected for all these years. We walked over to the picnic table and I picked her up and laid her on a blanket on the table and then sat on the bench and stroked her silky fur. We sat there for a long time "talking" about all the fun we'd had and all the hunting trips we'd had together. It was a beautiful spring day, with a warm breeze blowing, lots of birds singing and the flowers and leaves opening up. My heart was breaking. I was saying goodbye to my friend of 12 years.

Finally I heard the sound of Dr. Pat's truck as she pulled into the driveway. I walked around to the front of the house to let her know we were waiting out back. The time had come.

I sat back down and put my arms around Sally and said goodbye and in a couple of seconds she was gone. I don't know how long I sat there after Dr. Pat left but finally I got up and wrapped Sally in her blanket and buried her in the back garden next to her mother.

It was a long day. I had no ambition to do much of anything so I just sat and thought about having a dog and the pain of seeing them grow old and then having to say goodbye to them. I looked up from my daydreaming and saw Thunderfoot walking slowly across the yard. He came into the house and sat down but neither of us said a word.

"Can I get the picture book out?" he asked.

"Yeah, that might be a good idea," I said.

He got out my photo album and we sat side by side on the couch and paged through it. The first dog pictures were of old Bea. There were lots of those. Then there were pictures of Bea with her litter of puppies. Sally had been one of a litter of nine and the puppy pictures were enough to make us laugh.

"Gosh, you could sure tell which one was Sally," Thunderfoot said pointing to a puppy with a familiar look on her face. Sally always had a look of "attitude" even when she was a few weeks old. It was why I chose her over all the others.

"She was the boss of all the puppies," I said.

There were pictures of us fishing, Sally riding in the boat. In one she was sitting on the little platform on the bow, hanging out over the water. There were many with her swimming toward us with a tennis ball in her mouth. There was one of her eating birthday cake, and many more.

We laughed at the picture of Thunderfoot feeding Sally cake with a fork and getting frosting all over her nose.

We smiled at a picture of Thunderfoot and Sally both sleeping on the floor, his arms around her after a duck hunt. They were both still muddy from the swamp.

"She got to do a lot of stuff, didn't she?" he said.

"Yeah, she had a good life."

The more we looked the better we felt. Finally we came to the part of the book where Sophie started showing up. Sophie was asleep on the floor at our feet. "Do you think Soph knows what happened?" he asked.

"I don't think she understands death but you can tell she knows something is wrong," I said reaching down to pet Sophie.

"Hey Soph, want to go play ball?" Thunderfoot asked.

Sophie jumped to her feet and frantically began looking for a tennis ball. In a short time she ran back to us with two of them in her mouth and out they went to play ball.

I sat outside at the picnic table watching the two of them playing. After a while Sophie started getting tired. Thunderfoot walked over to the fresh ground where I had buried Sally.

He squatted down and patted the earth and said something and then took off across the yard toward his house. "I told her we won't ever forget her," he said.

We sure won't.

Goodbye Sally.

The Ice-Cream Fish

The johnboat was as silent as midnight in a cemetery. Thunderfoot, his friend Trent and I were fishing in the river bottoms for northerns. We were casting plugs and spinners to likely-looking places in hopes to be the first one in the boat to catch a fish. Normally there was a lot of conversation about everything from fishing to baseball, but right now, we were just starting out for the evening and there were no fish caught as of yet. Therefore, the ice-cream fish was still up for grabs.

I should explain. Somehow many fishing trips ago, we started a game in which the last person to catch his first fish of the trip had to buy ice-cream at the gas station on the way home. If it were just Thunderfoot and I, the first fish caught was the winner and the loser had to buy. If there were three people fishing, as there were today, the first two were eliminated and the third guy got the honors of buying.

It was serious business, not so much because of the price of the ice-cream but more for the prestige that came with being the non-loser. So, we were beating the water frothy as Thunderfoot reared back on his rod and set the hook into a mid-sized northern.

He looked to the back of the boat and got a smug look on his face. "I can't decide what flavor to have tonight," he said. Just then the northern jumped into the air and Thunderfoot's spinner-bait came flying back and hit him in the middle of the chest.

"That was close enough to count," he said quickly.

"No way, pal," Trent and I said simultaneously. "You didn't touch him, it doesn't count."

Thunderfoot looked wounded but it didn't take him long to start fishing again.

I picked up the paddle and moved us a short way down the lake so could fish some new territory. Everyone was working pretty hard for that first fish and the boys liked nothing more than to stick me with the ice-cream buying duties. We were drifting toward a spot on the lake where we always caught a northern. We called it "Ambush Point." It was a place where the weed lines from each side of the lake jutted out and almost met at mid-lake. It was a perfect ambush point for a predator fish like a northern to be lying in wait for a meal. The boys were watching it come into range but my end of the boat was closer so I had first crack at it.

I cast my spinner past the point and took about two turns on the reel when a northern smashed it and the fight was on.

"Oh, no!" Thunderfoot exclaimed. "Fall off! Fall off!"

But the fish stayed on and I worked it next to the boat, picked it up just behind the head and lifted it into the boat. "Behold," I said showing the fish to the boys. They were kind of sullen.

I removed the hook and dropped the fish over the side smiling sweetly to them. "I'll not be buying tonight," I said grinning at them.

Thunderfoot and Trent looked at each other and both cast to "Ambush Point" at the same time. Their baits landed about a foot apart and Trent's rod bent hard as a fish grabbed his spinner. He set the hook and began grinning as he fought the fish to the boat.

Thunderfoot sat there in disbelief watching as the fish got closer and closer. "Drop off, throw the hook," he urged. "Hand me something to cut the line."

Trent lifted the fish over the side of the boat and grabbed it in mid-air. Then he turned and smiled politely to Thunderfoot who was speechless.

Suddenly Trent got a funny look on his face and turned to me. "Which side of the mouth did you hook that fish you caught?"

"In the right side, right in the lip," I said.

"Look here," he said holding the fish so I could see it. Thunderfoot climbed over the seat to see also, and there in the left side of the fish's mouth was Trent's hook....and in the right side was a still bleeding hole where my bait had been just a couple of minutes earlier.

"That's the same fish I caught," I said laughing.

Trent and I laughed like crazy but Thunderfoot failed to see the humor.

"That can't be legal. He didn't catch a new fish, he caught the same one. That's not fair. We need some rule changes here I think."

Trent looked at me and said, "Chocolate or vanilla?"

Again, Thunderfoot failed to see why we thought this was so funny. We fished for another couple of hours and Thunderfoot grumbled the whole while about being cheated. Finally we loaded up and went to the local gas station for our ice-cream. We sat at a table and I ordered vanilla, Trent ordered chocolate and Thunderfoot had a twist. "Boy, this is the best ice-cream I've ever had," Trent exclaimed.

"Yeah, mine is really good too," I said.

"By the way, thanks for the ice-cream, buddy," Trent added to Thunderfoot.

"Yeah thanks..." I didn't finish. Thunderfoot was shooting death rays out of his eyes at me.

We finished up and Thunderfoot got up slowly and walked to the counter to pay for the ice-cream. He shoved his hand into his pocket and then began grinning. His hand came out of his pocket holding a nickel.

"Um, maybe I'll have to borrow about "2.95 from you," he said. "I seem to be a little short on funds."

It didn't bother me a bit. It was the principal that counted anyway.

Thanks, Thunderfoot.

The Smallmouth Caper

Thunderfoot and I were floating through the morning for on what had been planned to be a day of river fishing for smallmouth bass. He was grumbling about having to get up so early and rummaging around in my tackle box for *his* lucky lure.

"Where's my lucky pink Pop-R?" he asked.

"Did you look on the end of your pole?"

Big grin. "I didn't see it there. My eyes don't work so early in the morning."

He picked up his pole and his lucky bait and began casting toward the bank of the river. His second cast went right into the overhanging branches of one of the trees on shore. "Oh no....the Pink Lady is in the tree...Go back! Go back!"

I pulled on the starter rope and the engine roared to life. I put into gear and took us back upstream to where his lure was hanging in the tree. Thunderfoot stood up on the front seat of the boat and retrieved his lure. I cut the motor and cast behind an overhanging tree branch that looked like a good bass hideout and had a strike as soon as the bait hit the water. A nice-sized smallie jumped into the air and gave me a thrilling fight before coming alongside the boat to be lipped and released.

"Oh no, I buy again," Thunderfoot said.

"That is, if you have any money this time," I said. He grinned and cast the Pink Lady into another tree. About six trees later, Thunderfoot actually hit the water with his cast and got a good strike. He was so surprised that he jerked his bait back and missed the fish. I cast to the same spot and caught the fish as soon as my bait landed.

"Oh that's real cute," he said as I took the hook out of the fish and released it.

"You've got to be quick," I said smiling sweetly.

We fished another couple hundred yards of riverbank and I caught three more fish. I had just cast near a stump sticking out

47

of the water and missed a fish when the Pink Lady sailed past my head and landed in the same spot. The water exploded as the fish tried to eat the Pink Lady and Thunderfoot hauled back to set the hook. He missed the fish but his lure became airborne like a little pink bullet and flew back toward the boat as supersonic speed right at me. I just had time to duck to keep from being hit in the face. The Pink Lady imbedded herself in the top of my head with a crack.

"Watch out!" Thunderfoot yelled after the lure had hit me.

"Thanks for the warning," I said. I reached up to untangle the lure from my hair but it was stuck tight. "Come here and take a look at this," I said.

"Eeee-ouch!" he said as he parted the hair. He looked carefully and the said, "I think I'll need the needle nose pliers."

"Wait! What do you mean?" I said. "I'm not sure I want you operating on my head using some pliers."

"Well, it's either that or you'll be wearing the Pink Lady for a barrette for the rest of the day."

I wasn't so sure which scared me worst, the idea of Thunderfoot operating on my head or the fact that he knew what a barrette was. But, it was too early in the day for me to think about having a fish hook stuck in my head all day so I agreed to let him work on me.

Thunderfoot took the needle nose and gripped the hook with it. "The front treble hook has two of the three stuck in your head," he said. "The back hook is free, so I'll just get hold of it and give it a jerk. Ready?"

"Ready."

He took a deep breath and jerked the hooks from my scalp. At the same time the front hook popped out of my skin, the back hook imbedded itself in the skin of my forehead about half way down between my hairline and my eyebrows.

"Whoops," Thunderfoot said. "That one's pretty shallow. It'll come out easy."

He grabbed the lure and plucked it from my forehead like

picking a grape off a bunch. Then he checked his precious Pink Lacy for damage. "I hope your hard head didn't dull my hooks," he said grinning.

I was wiping blood from my forehead as the bait whizzed past my head again and right into a tree. I just shook my head and started the motor.

We fished pretty uneventfully for about three hours. I caught and released about a dozen smallies and Thunderfoot caught and released about a dozen trees. We were getting close to where he had left the truck that morning when Thunderfoot let out a whoop and the biggest smallmouth of the day jumped from the water with his Pink Lady sticking out of his mouth. He fought the fish nicely, and finally lipped it and held it up for me to see. It was a beauty, so I grabbed the camera and snapped a picture of him holding the fish and grinning.

He released the fish and said, "I don't catch a lot of them but I go for quality."

He turned toward the shore and promptly cast his Pink Lady into a tree. "Sometimes the Lady is a tree lover," he joked. "My specialty is trees, yours if fish."

I shook my head and started the motor to go back to fetch his bait. What a dull day it would have been with out him and his Pink Lady. I would have had to just fish all day long.

How boring.

Thanks, Thunderfoot.

Say Pull

"Bring your shotgun over and we'll go and do some trapshooting," I said to Thunderfoot over the phone. "And bring some of those shells I gave you."

A few minutes later Thunderfoot came through the door with his twelve-gauge shotgun and a zip-lock bag with four shotgun shells inside. "This is all the shells I had left. Is this enough?"

I looked over at him. He gave me a pitiful look. "I left three boxes of light loads in the ammunition box the last time we went shooting," I said. "Where did they go?"

"Well, I was up at Grandpa's and I was trying to shoot down a tree, and I kinda used them all up."

I didn't even bother to ask why he was trying to shoot down a tree. "Well, go look in the shell drawer of the gun cabinet and see what's left."

He opened the drawer and began opening boxes of shells piling loose ones up into sorted piles on the floor until he had accumulated about a hundred of them. "We got plenty," he said brightly.

I looked at the shells and began eliminating some of them. "These are steel-shot, they're too expensive to shoot at clay birds. These are heavy magnums for turkeys and geese. They're shoulder breakers, leave them here too. The rest are ok, bag them up."

"How come we can't take those magnums, they'll really break those clay pigeons."

"They'll also break your shoulder. They've got two ounces of shot and the maximum load of powder. I don't want to get the snot kicked out of me."

"Ok, we'll leave them then," he said.

We loaded up the trap, the guns and shells into the pickup and drove down to our shooting range, an old lagoon that was dried up and filled with tall grass. It was a good place to shoot because the walls of the lagoon served as a backstop to stop our stray pellets and the tall grass cushioned the fall of the clay pigeons we missed. After shooting a while, we could go and find the intact birds and "refly" them, to use Thunderfoot's term. When we got to the lagoon we set up the trap and uncased our guns.

"Let's shoot a group of five each and take turns until we've each shot at twenty-five birds. Then we'll see who's got the best score," he said. "And the loser gets to buy an ice-cream on the way home." He looked pretty confident, so I agreed and he even volunteered to go first.

He put one shell in his gun and got ready. I sat down at the trap and loaded a clay pigeon onto the throwing arm.

"Ok, go!" he said.

"You have to say pull."

"What? Pull? What do you mean pull? Why not ok go?"

"I don't know why," I said. "That's what they say...pull."

"Well that seems kind of silly."

I just looked at him.

"Jeez...ok, pull."

I pulled the string attached to the arm, launching the bird into the air. Thunderfoot swung the gun to the bird, pulled the trigger, and completely obliterated it. I gaped at him, a look of wonder on my face. He looked smugly at me, opened the breech of the gun, blew the smoke out of the end of the barrel, dropped another shell in and closed the breech. He broke three of the next four and then swaggered over to the tailgate of the truck and laid his gun down on the opened case. I got up from the trap, slightly stunned, and picked up my gun for my turn at shooting. "You must have been practicing," I said.

"Just natural ability," he said grinning.

I got ready and said, "Pull." The bird flew up and I missed it cleanly. I didn't even look his way because I could hear him snickering as I slipped another shell into the gun. My next four shots were good hits, so I felt a little better as Thunderfoot stepped up for his second turn.

This time he was a bit overconfident and only broke three of his next five birds. His swagger was less pronounced as he put his gun down and took his place at the trap. My second set was as good as my first. I broke four out of five birds giving me a lead of eight to seven.

Thunderfoot broke three on his third set and so did I so I still had a one bird lead. But, the fourth set proved good for both of us again and we each broke four birds. I still held my one bird lead going into the last set.

"This is it," I said. "I lead by one going into the last set." He ignored me and stepped up to shoot. His first shot was good. His second was also good.....two for two. He wouldn't even look at me. He was concentrating as hard as I had ever seen him concentrate. He broke the next two in a row. He had one more chance to break all five. "Pull," he said. I pulled the string and the last bird disintegrated in a puff of black smoke. Thunderfoot turned and looked at me with an evil grin. "Don't miss," he said.

If I hit all five I would win. If I missed one, we tied. But horror of horrors, if I missed two...I didn't even want to think about it.

I powdered number one and two. As the third bird came off the trap I overshot and missed it cleanly. I could hear him snickering but I didn't look. I bent down to get another shell from the box on the ground but the box was empty. "Do you have any more shells?" I asked.

"Oh yeah, I've got two in my pocket," he said reaching his hand out for my gun. I handed it to him and he loaded it for me. "What a nice thing to do," I thought.

I got ready and gave the pull command. The bird came into my field of view and I swung the gun on it. As the front sight passed the bird, I pulled the trigger expecting the light recoil from the minimally loaded trap shell. Instead, I nearly fell over backward as the blast from the gun nearly broke my shoulder. There was a great cloud of smoke, as the clay bird disintegrated. My right thumb which was gripped across the stock had hammered back with the recoil and slammed into the end of my nose, causing a great flood of tears to flow from my eyes. I shook my head to clear it, bewildered by what had just happened. I heard a braying noise like a hyena coming from the tall grass behind me. When I turned around all I saw of Thunderfoot were his tennis shoes sticking up from the grass. He was lying on his back laughing his fool head off.

"What the heck was that?" I said as I opened the chamber on the gun and ejected the spent shell casing. I stooped over and picked up the empty. It was a three-inch magnum goose shell.

"Oops, how did that get in there?" Thunderfoot said falling back in another fit of laughter.

I wiped my eyes as he got up from the grass. He was staggering around like a drunkard laughing crazily. He reached in his pocket and handed me his last shell. I carefully checked to ensure that it was a light load and put it into the gun.

"We're tied now," he said. "Don't choke."

I got ready and raised the gun. "Pull," I said.

No bird. I looked over at him.

"What?" he said.

"Did you forget how to work that thing?" I asked.

"Oh did you say pull? Sorry I didn't hear you."

I got ready again and I could hear him snickering.

"Pull!"

The bird came out to my left and swung to the right. I got the front sight on it and followed, passed through, and pulled the trigger. The bird sailed out into the grass and disappeared untouched.

"Nice shot!" Hideous laughter.

He was on his back in the grass again. "I make that to be a score of 18 for you and 19 for me...I'll have vanilla."

"You're not going to take a win after you sabotaged me with that magnum shell are you?"

He grinned at me and said, "That was simply an oversight on my part. I'm really sorry that happened. By the way...did I mention that I'll have vanilla?"

Thanks, Thunderfoot.

The Mallard Hilton

"I need one of those old bus seats," Thunderfoot said as he hurried through the back door. "I'm building us a new duck blind."

"We have a duck blind," I said looking up from my newspaper.

"Yeah, I know, but I'm going to build this one for the L pond. That way we'll be able to get some of those late season mallards that are always landing in there."

The L pond was a short way from our present duck blind and named L pond because it was shaped like a backwards L. Last duck season we had watched helplessly as dozens of late season mallards and wood ducks landed in the pond every day we hunted. Unfortunately we had made the mistake of trying to get to the ducks several times....always with the same results. We came back from the L pond wet, muddy, and without ducks.

The problem was that the L pond was situated in the middle of a floating bog. The marsh grass growing there was only about two to three feet tall for about the last twenty yards on all sides of the pond. Sneaking up on the pond was as close to impossible as it could be due to the fact that the whole area was floating and there was no cover. Every step you took made the floating mass sway and rock and eventually you got to a place where there was nowhere safe to put your foot next and you ended up breaking through the floating grass and sinking into the mud underneath. Unfortunately the mud underneath was deeper than your hip boots would tolerate and you ended up with a boot, or sometimes both boots full of water and mud. Of course, the commotion of one of us dropping through the bog gave away our presence and the ducks flew away. It was a good place for ducks and a very bad place for humans. I had to admit it was a great place to put a duck blind but I was not convinced that we could accomplish such a task.

"How will we get a duck blind on the L pond?" I asked.

"Leave that to me. Now, can I have the bus seat or not?"

I relented and we went to the garage where I helped him drag a bus seat down from the rafters. I had stored them there several years earlier when I had heard that the school was replacing seats in some of the busses. I had learned that the old seats could be purchased for two dollars each, so I bought a couple of them. I really had no idea what I'd use them for but for two bucks I couldn't pass them up. As it turned out, we used one in our first duck blind and it made a great place to sit while waiting for ducks.

I offered to help him carry the seat over to his house but he told me he had everything under control. He took off carrying and dragging the seat across the back yard and I stood and watched him. I had to grin as he struggled with the seat. He did put himself into a project when he got an idea into his head.

I didn't see much of him for the next few days and kind of forgot about the duck blind. Then one day after school he came strutting in the front door and announced that the new duck blind was ready to go. I was required to follow him to his house for an inspection of his work. Off we went to his house and as I rounded the corner of the house I stopped in my tracks and gazed in amazement at the structure sitting in his yard.

The thing had the general shape of a duck blind with the front side lower than the back and a partial roof over the back side, similar to our other blind. The whole thing was covered in chicken wire and he had tied bundles of marsh grass to the wire which made the thing look like a grass covered outhouse, only a little longer than a normal outhouse would be. There was no floor in the thing but what I guessed was the floor was sitting by itself a short way away on the grass. The part that was quite amazing was the size of the thing. It was big enough to put in roosts and nests and use as a chicken coop. There was room for three hunters...possibly four if you were all good friends.

"Good Lord! How do you plan on getting that thing to the pond?" I asked.

"I've got that all figured out," Thunderfoot responded. "We'll just go out to the pond in the canoe and pound posts into the mud exactly where I measure. Then we'll take the floor out with the canoe and slide it out onto the posts and nail it down. Then we'll go back and get the blind and take it out and slide it off the canoe onto the floor. All we have to do then is put a few nails into the floor through the blind and presto...The Mallard Hilton." He acted as if I was completely dense for not seeing the simplicity of the plan on my own.

Well, I had to look this over, so I walked up and inspected the blind. I grabbed the corner and tried to lift. "Wow, that thing must weigh three hundred pounds," I said looking at him incredulously.

"Ahh, no way. Trust me. This'll work," he said gathering up the posts and tools we were going to need. "I figure we can take the bottom out tonight and then tomorrow we can take the blind and finish up, since I don't have school."

I wasn't as confident as he was but I agreed, so we loaded up all the materials and drove down to the marsh. We parked as close to the pond as we could get and then carried the canoe through the brush to the high bank and then down to the marsh. We made another trip for 4 x 4 posts, a bag of nails, a hammer, a sledgehammer and my small chain saw. One more trip was required to manhandle the floor section through the brush and onto the canoe. By the time the two of us got in, the canoe was very close to being overloaded and was very unstable.

We pushed off through the marsh grass and worked our way to the L pond. A while later Thunderfoot stood up to survey the area to choose a spot for the blind. He nearly capsized us when he stood but soon he sat down and we maneuvered to where he had decided would be the best place for the blind. Thunderfoot stood again and placed one of the 4 x 4 posts into the pond and shoved it down into the mud. Then he picked up the sledge hammer and began to pound the post down into the bottom of the pond. His first swing nearly tipped us over. He turned to me with a silly grin on his face. "I guess one of us will have to get into the water to do this. We'll tip the canoe over if we try to do it from here. I'm gonna be too short if I'm in the water, so I guess..."

Somehow I knew this was coming already. I had never been to the L pond in my duck hunting career and left it dry, so there wasn't any reason why I should expect to leave dry today either. I slid out over the side of the canoe and the water came to just about six inches over the tops of my hip boots. I nodded as the cold water filled my boots. Yeah, this was pretty much what I'd expected. I gave Thunderfoot an evil eye as I began hammering the first post into the hard packed mud at the bottom of the pond. About three thousand sledge hammer hits later I had all the posts driven into the mud in the precise places Thunderfoot directed them. I was verging on heart failure, sweating and panting. Thunderfoot was taking careful measurements from the dry canoe and marking each post with a pencil as to the right height for them to be cut off.

"Now if you can just cut on those lines, we can slide the floor over the posts and the bottom of the blind will be all done," he said cheerily.

He was very cool and calm sitting there in the canoe. I, on the other hand, was standing in muddy water, soaked to the skin from sweat and panting like a dog in August. I took the chainsaw and began cutting off the tops of the posts. It didn't take long for me to become covered in sawdust as it stuck to my sweaty body. I finished and handed the saw back to Thunderfoot who was smiling and nodding at my good work.

"Jeez, you look like a snowman," he observed. "Well, let's get the floor nailed down before the mosquitoes get bad."

We slid the floor off the canoe and onto the posts and with a little adjustment it dropped into place. Thunderfoot stepped out onto it and began nailing it down and then stood up proudly to survey his creation. "Looks good," he said. "See, I told you this wouldn't be so hard."

I managed to get myself back into the canoe and we paddled back to the shore. We left the canoe and tools there for the next phase of construction and headed home.

The next day we manhandled the chicken coop into the truck and somehow drug it through the brush to the high bank. We slid it down to the pond and got it onto the canoe. The canoe was still floating but just barely. There was very little freeboard as we paddled the monstrosity toward the floor waiting on the pond. Miraculously we made it to the floor without sinking the canoe. As we got to the platform, Thunderfoot stood up and stepped out onto the floor. When his weight was removed from the front of the canoe, the back became too heavy to keep the thing floating and within a second of him leaving, the chicken coop and I went straight to the bottom.

Of course, the blind slid back onto me and I had a heck of a time getting up and out from under it. Meanwhile Thunderfoot was shouting at me. "Watch out for the grass! Don't ruin the grass on the blind!"

This time I was wet all the way to the top of my head, something I hadn't previously experienced at the L pond. But of course, Thunderfoot was bone dry. I managed to get one end of the blind onto the platform and we manhandled the monster into place. It fit like a glove. "Not a bad piece of engineering," he said strutting. "I told you this would be a piece of cake." He took the small hammer and nailed down the blind to the floor and then put the bus seat into place.

Then he removed a newspaper covered board that he had put into the bottom of the canoe earlier. He took the paper off and nailed the pine board to the blind wall. He stood back and read what was written on the board: "The Mallard Hilton. Owned by Dan and Thunderfoot...Duck Hunting Buds."

For some reason the mud oozing around in my boots didn't seem so bad after all.

Thanks, Thunderfoot.

A Little Buck Fever?

Thunderfoot and I were cleaning up after the close of the duck season. We had brought the gear home from the duck blind and now were untangling decoy lines and sorting the decoys into piles of like ducks for storage in burlap bags in my garage. We were one week away from the deer gun season. Thunderfoot had been fretting all week about getting ready for deer hunting, so he was working extra hard to get the duck stuff put away quickly.

"I think we should be out shooting the deer guns and not fooling around with this duck stuff," he said.

"Yeah, and then the duck stuff will be in a big mess on the floor for the rest of the winter. Just get this done and we'll go shoot our guns, we've got plenty of time."

"Well, I want to be right on when that big trophy comes past me," he said.

We finally finished with the duck gear and I got the deer rifles from the gun cabinet while Thunderfoot found some paper targets. We headed down to the old lagoon to sight-in the guns. A lot of other hunters used the old lagoon too, so there was a backstop someone had built as a place to hang your target, and a wooden spool that highline wire had been on for a table to use as a shooting rest.

Thunderfoot sprinted over to the backstop and pinned up a couple of targets as I uncased the guns.

"You go first," he said.

Normally he was the first to do any shooting. He loved shooting any gun, at anything, be it targets, ducks, pigeons, whatever, but now he wanted me to go first. I figured that he might be a little afraid of the recoil of the deer guns. He didn't have a deer rifle of his own, so I lent him one of mine and he hadn't shot it before today.

I folded up my gun case for a rest, knelt behind the wire spool and sighted through the scope of my 30.06 rifle. I carefully zeroed in the crosshairs on the center of the target and squeezed the trigger. Thunderfoot almost jumped out of his shoes when the gun went off.

"Wow! That's loud. Does it kick hard?"

"No...it's no worse than a 12-gauge, it just sounds worse."

I shot a couple more times and then we walked over to the target so see how I did. All three of my shots were in a circle the size of a silver dollar so I was pretty confident I could hit a deer where I wanted.

We went back to the spool and Thunderfoot carefully slid a cartridge into the .270 I had loaned him. "Now just aim careful and squeeze," I said. "Don't worry about the recoil."

He sighted for a long time and then pulled the trigger. He jumped about a foot when the gun went off. "Holy cow! It kicks like a horse!" he said rubbing his shoulder.

"Oh come on," I said. "It's not that bad, just quit worrying about the recoil and you'll be fine."

He shot again and jumped just as badly.

"You're anticipating the kick and jumping before it even goes off," I said. "Go put up another target and try again."

He trotted out to the backstop and while he was busy, I opened the breech of the gun and removed the live shell and replaced it with an empty. He came back, picked up the gun and sighted again. He took a deep breath and squeezed the trigger. When the gun went *click* he jumped a foot.

What the...what happened?" he asked.

I held my hand out for the gun and he handed it to me. I opened the chamber and took out the empty shell. "See? You're jumping for nothing. You jumped even without a shell going off. Now put in a live one and quit being such a baby about the recoil."

He gave me a look with the baby crack but then grinned. "Ok, maybe you are right," he said.

From then on, he shot like a pro.

The next afternoon we headed out to the farm where we were going to hunt. I had obtained permission from the owner a few weeks earlier and I wanted Thunderfoot to get the lay of the land before opening morning. That way he'd know where everything was and where I wanted him to stand opening morning.

"Ken told me he's been seeing a huge buck up here all summer," I said as we walked up the ridge road to the top of the hill. Just as I said it a nice buck and three does jumped up from a ditch and trotted up the side of the hill ahead of us.

"Wow! I don't think I can wait until next week," Thunderfoot said as he watched the deer go over the hill.

When we got to the top I took him to the place where I planned on him standing opening day and showed him around. Then we walked up to where I was going to stand. I had given him the best spot on the farm. My spot was above him on the hill where I could keep an eye on him.

The next week was a long one for Thunderfoot. He was at my house every night talking deer stories and hauling gear over. By the middle of the week he had brought over so many clothes that it looked like I was having a garage sale.

Finally Friday evening came and he showed up after school with his lunch packed for the next day. He slept in the spare room and went to bed at eight o'clock so he'd be ready for an early start in the morning.

The next morning we were at our stands on the hill about an hour before shooting time. I wanted to get to the farm early so we could get situated before other hunters on surrounding lands would begin arriving. This way they would move some deer toward us and not the other way around. We were the only ones hunting this farm, so we didn't have any competition from anyone close to us.

The darkness began to fade. Soon I was able to make out shapes. A short time later the shapes began to turn into real objects that began to take color and form. I looked down the hill and saw Thunderfoot at rigid attention as he watched a deer path below his stand.

From far away I heard the first shot of the season and soon there was another not so far away. In the next few minutes shots rang out all around us as hunters saw their first deer of the day. There was no movement in our woods for almost an hour. Finally I saw a doe working her way down the hillside toward Thunderfoot. He had told me he wasn't going to shoot a doe but was going for a trophy buck. He did have a permit for a doe, so I wondered what he'd do when he saw the deer. He slowly raised the gun and looked at the doe in the scope then lowered it again. Then he raised it, hesitated, and lowered it again as the doe walked away.

A while later I saw him raise his gun again and I looked in the direction he was aiming. There was a fork buck with two points on each side standing about eighty yards from him in the field. He held the gun up for a long time before he lowered it. The buck walked off into the woods and Thunderfoot began to pace around.

At noon he came up to my stand and sat down on the ground beside me to help me eat my lunch. "What happened to your food?" I asked.

"Oh that was gone a long time ago," he said.

"Why didn't you shoot that four –pointer?" I asked.

"I was going to but then I thought maybe I should wait for a bigger one."

"Well, don't wait too long," I said.

He went back to his stand and I settled down to wait for the afternoon action. It didn't take long until a bunch of does and a six-point buck trotted up near Thunderfoot. He again raised his gun, watched them for a while and let them go.

I noticed movement a short time later and turned to see a nice four-pointer standing below me. I knew he wasn't going up to Thunderfoot and a trophy wasn't a priority for me, so I raised my gun and fired. The buck took one step and dropped in his tracks. I laid my gun down and started walking toward the deer, but Thunderfoot passed me on the run.

"Holy cow! You got him!" he panted. "He's not a trophy but he's a nice one."

As we field dressed the deer I asked him about the six-pointer he had passed up.

"Too many does in the way," he said. "Well, I've got to get back to my stand, see you at quittin' time."

I cleaned up and settled back to wait for the end of the day. I had almost fallen asleep when I noticed something coming across the woods toward Thunderfoot. There was a huge buck and four does trotting right at him, but he wouldn't see them coming because he was too far down the hill. Finally they crested the ridge and he could see them. He raised the gun...lowered it...raised it...lowered it...and finally raised it a third time. All of the movement spooked the deer and they turned and headed back the way they had come.

Thunderfoot was stomping his feet and kicking the ground and I could see little puffs of steam coming out of his mouth as he cussed. I grinned to myself.

When quitting time finally came I dragged my deer down to his level. He walked over to me. "Get a little buck fever?" I asked.

"No!"

"That's ok, it happens to a lot of people," I said.

"I did *not* have buck fever," he said indignantly. "The does came out in the open but the buck stayed back far enough that I couldn't get a good shot at him. All I could see was his head."

"Why didn't you shoot him in the head?"

"Are you crazy? I would have ruined the trophy rack,"

Yeah right.

Thanks, Thunderfoot.

Watch Out for Trains

Thunderfoot and I were heading out on the first ice fishing trip of the year. We had an early freeze-up in the fall and the ice was good in most of the places we liked to fish. Consequently as soon as the deer season was finished we had to get out for a day of ice fishing.

Thunderfoot had been ready for days and could hardly wait to get going. "Where are we going to try?" he asked.

"I don't know," I replied. "We'll just drive along the road up the Mississippi and watch for a bunch of people fishing. That should be the hot spot."

"Huh?"

"A place where there are a lot of fishermen is usually where there are a lot of fish too," I said.

That seemed to satisfy him because he slid down in the seat and took a nap as I drove along the highway. A while later I noticed a lot of cars parked along the railroad tracks up ahead, so I slowed down and pulled onto the shoulder of the road. I watched the fishermen and they were all pretty intent on their fishing. Few were wandering around or visiting which led me to believe the fish were biting. Soon I saw one lift a fish from a hole and then another did the same thing.

"Are we here?" Thunderfoot asked yawning and stretching.

"It looks like they're catching some fish over there," I said pointing to the backwater. "Let's give it a try here."

He was out of the truck like a shot and started gathering up gear and piling it up on the gravel along the highway. "How are we going to get over the railroad tracks?" he asked looking down at the ten foot embankment below us.

"I guess we'll have to take a little at a time and then come back and make another trip until we get it all down there," I said.

We hauled the buckets filled with poles and lunch over the tracks and then went back and got the sled, the heater, and the rest of the gear. Once we had everything on the ice we loaded it all on the sled and took off for the cluster of fishermen.

We drilled holes a short way from the others and I had hardly gotten the ice chips strained out of my holes when Thunderfoot let out a whoop and lifted a huge bluegill onto the ice. It had no more than hit the ice when I got a bite and caught its twin.

"The hot spot," he said grinning from ear to ear.

The action was just about non-stop. In the next couple of hours we caught fish one after the other until we had a pretty good pile of them on the ice.

"We better count these fish to make sure we don't go over our limit," I said.

"You count...I'll fish."

I started counting the fish and putting them into the buckets as I counted. One bucket was full and the other almost half-full when I got to number ninety-four. "Six more and we have to quit," I said.

"You mean five," he said hoisting another fish from his hole.

It only took a few more minutes and we had out one hundredth fish. "I can't believe we have to quit," he said sadly.

"I hate to quit too, but that's the way it is. Besides, I'm getting hungry and I know a place up the road that makes hamburgers the size of small meat-loafs."

He perked up at that and we loaded the gear onto the sled with the buckets of fish. When we got to the tracks he began surveying the situation. "If I got up a little way and took the rope that's on the sled, we could probably just slide everything up in one trip and not have to go up and then down and then up again."

"I don't know," I said. "It's pretty steep."

"I'll pull, you push," he said as he scrambled up the rocky, steep slope. I still wasn't too sure about this but if it worked it would save us a lot of time and climbing, so I got down and began pushing on the back of the sled. Thunderfoot was up ahead pulling and although our progress was slow, we did begin to get up the hill. We were about halfway up when Thunderfoot looked

65

over his shoulder and let go of the rope. The sled suddenly got very heavy and began pushing back at me. I began backing down the hill quite fast and within a couple of seconds the sled ran over me and I went over backwards to the bottom. When the sled ran me over, the buckets of fish spilled and when we stopped moving at the bottom, I was covered with one hundred slippery bluegills.

I lay on the ice with the slimy mess in my lap and lifted the sled off me. Suddenly I heard a familiar snickering coming from farther up the hill. "Watch out! There's a train coming," he said as he hustled down the bank.

Sure enough a train was coming. We weren't in any danger but it got pretty loud and windy for several minutes while the train thundered past us.

"Boy it's a good thing I saw that train coming and let the rope go so we weren't on the tracks," he said.

"What? You let the sled go on purpose?"

"Well sure....I didn't want the gear and the fish to get run over, and I didn't want you to get run over, and I sure didn't want me to get run over," he said.

"Did you ever think to just sit still and wait for it to pass?"

"It was pretty scary up there. You know, I heard about trains coming along and sucking people right under them. You're pretty big and heavy but I'm just a little guy and I didn't want to die."

Well, you couldn't argue with logic like that.

Thanks, Thunderfoot.

Persistence Pays

Thunderfoot had been pestering me all week to take him northern fishing. The problem was that he wanted to go to a slough we had fished the past summer that was deep in the marsh. It was fine earlier in the winter when the marsh was frozen solid but now it was early spring and the trip to the lake was over some very shaky ground.

"What do you mean we can't get there?" he asked.

"I mean that we can't get there because that marsh is full of springs and we'll get wet if we try to cross it."

"But think of all those big northerns out there just licking their lips waiting for us," he said grinning.

Against my better judgment, I gave in and about an hour later I was carefully stepping from clump of frozen swamp grass to clump of frozen swamp grass. I worked my way very carefully toward the lake while skinny little Thunderfoot abandoned me and took off across the marsh without a problem. He was waiting for me on the frozen lake.

"Hurry up with the shiners" he said as he drilled his third hole.

Somehow I made it to the lake without falling through and the lake ice was thick enough to make me feel pretty safe. I handed Thunderfoot the minnow bucket and he took off to bait up the tip-ups.

"Last one to catch a northern has to clean the fish!" he shouted over his shoulder. That was a pretty good deal for him especially since he already had his holes drilled and his tip-ups baited and was already fishing. I was still standing there with my tip-ups in my bucket, but I agreed anyway.

I was working on my second fishing-hole when he let out a whoop and took off for his far tip-up. The flag was up. He carefully lifted the tip-up from the hole, played out the line like a professional, waited for the fish to run and then jerked hard on the line. He pulled in a bare hook.

"Nuts...he got my shiner," he said. He ran back and grabbed the minnow bucket so he could re-bait his hook. He had barely gotten the tip-up back in the hole when the flag went up again. This time he waited even longer. Then he set the hook and the fish jerked him back nearly pulling him to the ice.

"He's a monster," he said as he pulled on the line. "Get over here and help..."

He never finished the sentence because the line broke. He pulled it in with a look of deep disappointment on his face. He came over to my tackle box and dug around until he found another steel leader, tied it onto his line, added a new hook and went back and baited the new rig and re-set the tip-up.

He hadn't walked fifteen feet from the tip-up when the flag went up again. This time he waited the appropriate amount of time and again hooked into a good-sized fish. He was working it toward the hole when the line went slack. He looked dejected as he pulled it from the hole.'

"He broke the leader." He began walking back toward me. "What kind of junk leaders do you buy anyway?"

I reminded him that if he didn't like the quality of my leaders he should purchase some of his own. He looked up from my tackle box in disbelief.

"You're out of leaders! Now what should I do?"

"Pull up one of your other tip-ups and use that one," I said.

"No way! I'll just tie the hook on without a leader. I don't want to give you the advantage by being one tip-up short."

He got everything set and we waited for about a half hour with no action. Suddenly Thunderfoot let out a yell and took off again for the same hole. "He's back! Bring the gaff and help me."

I doubted that it was the same fish but I thought it would be a good idea to help with a leaderless line on the tip-up. When I got to the hole he was working the fish, giving it line when it ran and carefully pulling when it gave a little. We finally got a look at it as it went past the hole. It was a big one. Thunderfoot pulled again and the fish turned and he got the head started up the hole. It looked to be at least a ten pound northern. I slipped the gaff into the fish's mouth and pulled it up onto the ice.

"All right! I got him! Look, my other lines are in his mouth."

I couldn't believe it. He was right. The first hook and leader, the second hook and broken leader, and the leaderless hook that caught the fish were all right there inside the mouth.

It was almost dark, so we packed up and started across the marsh to the truck. This time I wasn't so lucky. As I stepped onto a safe-looking spot, my foot went through up to my knee. When I tried to free my wet foot I broke through with the second foot. There I stood up to my knees in smelly swamp mud, holding my bucket and the auger.

Thunderfoot stopped and looked back at me. "Quit fooling around," he said. "I want to get back and see if that first minnow is in this fish's stomach. Be sure you look carefully when you clean him."

Thanks, Thunderfoot.

 Last Ice

It was one of those spring mornings that you dream about all winter. The sun was shining and the temperature was in the thirties by dawn. I was sitting at the kitchen table reading the morning newspaper when something caught my attention. As I looked up, I saw Thunderfoot crossing the back yard carrying his ice-fishing bucket and a sack that looked like a lunch sack. He was heading straight for my back door.

"She's a beauty today. I think we should go ice-fishing one more time," he said as he stuck his head into my refrigerator.

It's been pretty warm," I said. "Do you think the ice will still be safe?"

He looked at me with one of his "give me a break" looks. "Sure it's ok...if you're worried, I'll go first to test it."

That was real generous of him. Of course, he only weighed about a hundred pounds with his pockets full of sinkers, so he wasn't the one I was worried about. I weighed in at a higher weight bracket and was the one likely to take a drink, but it was such a beautiful day that I gave in and soon we were driving to the river bottoms.

Our first choice of lakes had about four feet of open water between the shore and the ice. We stood there looking out and I said, "Well, that's it. We can't get to the ice."

"How about Puffenrot's lake?" he said. "It's shady there where the trees are along the lake. The ice should be better there."

We drove a mile or so west and Thunderfoot had been right. The ice was solid right up to the shoreline, so he walked out to test it. When he jumped up and down the whole area shook and water splashed up in the old ice holes scattered around. "No problem," he said grinning.

I took the auger and drilled a hole. There was still about six inches of ice, but it was like packed snow, not good hard ice. The spring rains and higher angle of the sun had rotted the ice and it didn't look safe to me.

"Boy, I don't know…it's pretty soft," I said.

"Oh, come on. Don't be such a baby."

I gave in and we got the gear from the truck and started out to the main part of the lake. This particular lake is one of the few that is situated close to the high bank. The lake has a narrow arm that runs right up to the shore instead of the whole lake being in the middle of the marsh as are all the others in the area. The "arm" of water was the way to the lake since the marsh was mostly melted, so this was probably the only one we could get to.

Thunderfoot walked ahead of me with the minnows and his ice-bucket. I started walking out but stopped as the water in the old ice-holes began sloshing with each step.

I jumped up and down carefully and the whole thing was shaking. For some reason I decided to walk closer to the marsh on the shore side of the channel. I only took three steps when I went through.

At first it wasn't so terrible. The water was only about waist deep and I was standing on a sand bottom. It only took a few seconds though for the water to penetrate my clothes and run into my boots making it much more terrible very quickly.

I mistakenly tried to get back up on the ice by going closer to the marsh grass and broke through again several times before I realized my mistake and turned toward the middle where the ice was thicker. I tried several more times to climb up onto the ice but each time I broke through again. Suddenly I heard a choking sound and looked over at Thunderfoot who was lying on his back on the ice clutching his stomach and laughing hysterically, tears running down his face. "I suppose you'll want to go home now," he said sobbing with glee.

"Real funny…come here and take my buckets, so I can get out."

"No way! I'm not coming near you, I'll fall in too. Slide your buckets across the ice to me."

He sat down on his bucket to watch the show. "Try not to get the lunch wet will you?" he said laughing his fool head off.

71

I wallowed around back and forth like an elephant seal trying to get up on the beach and finally found some ice that I held me. I slid up on my belly and laid there completely exhausted. I was drenched from head to toe by ice cold water and smelled like a swamp, covered in grass and seaweed.

"Thanks for all the help," I said as I got to my feet.

"That was so funny. I'm sorry but I just couldn't keep from laughing," he said.

He gave me one of his impish grins and I had to smile. I suppose it had been a pretty good show at that. But I was beginning to get cold real fast, so I picked up my gear and turned to go back to the shore. It was then that I realized that the ice that connected the lake to the shore was now open water instead of ice. I also realized that Thunderfoot was now on the wrong side of the open water to be able to get to the shore. He must have read my thoughts because he stopped laughing and looked over at me. "Hey, you broke all the ice. How am I gonna get back?"

It was my turn to grin.

Thanks, Thunderfoot.

The Flying Fish

The ice went out below the dam last night," Thunderfoot said as he came through the door. "We better go and try for some walleyes from the shore." He was carrying his rod and reel and nodding his head up and down.

It didn't take much convincing to get me to go walleye fishing and not very long later we were climbing down over the bank to the sandy shore of the river, below the dam. We weren't the only ones with the idea of walleye fishing as many others had been keeping an eye on the ice, waiting for it to leave the water open.

Two old river-rats were leaving just as we walked down to the shore, so we took over their spot. Just above us were a couple of teenage boys who Thunderfoot knew and waved to and below us were a couple of other fishermen who we didn't know. The two teens were packing up and as they left, a family of African-American folks came walking down to the river bank. They took over the turf vacated by the teens. The family included a mom and dad, a young boy and an old lady that was obviously the grandma. The old lady was all decked out in a long coat and a thing on her head that looked like a turban. I thought it looked like she was on her way to church and had stopped off to fish. She was wearing a pair of knee length black rubber boots to complete her ensemble. I had to smile as she baited her hook and cast out her line. She let the bait settle and then held the pole in her hand staring intently at the tip waiting for a bite.

I put a minnow on my jig and cast out to the deeper water and let my jig sink to the bottom. When it touched bottom I lifted it and swam it back a little way toward me. As it touched again, I lifted and swam, lifted and swam. On about the fifth lift, I felt a little tic and set the hook into a nice "eating-sized" walleye. As I was putting it on the stringer Thunderfoot set the hook and reeled in a sheephead.

"Try a minnow," I said. "You'll get more walleyes. Those

sheephead will pester you all day if you use worms."

"I don't like to reach into that cold water for a minnow. I'm going to stick with crawlers," he said.

Well within half an hour I had three more nice walleyes on the stringer and Thunderfoot had beached six sheephead. He was just reeling in his seventh one when we heard a commotion on the shore above us as the dad from the family landed a huge northern.

"Wow," Thunderfoot said. "I didn't know there were northerns in here."

"Yeah, they're here now too," I said.

He took off the six inch sheephead that was on his hook and put it in the minnow bucket. "I need a bigger hook," he said digging into my tackle box. He must have found what he was looking for because he sat down cross-legged in the sand and began re-rigging his line. A minute later he fished around in the minnow bucket and pulled out the sheephead. "I'm gonna put this sheephead on the line as bait and catch me one of those big northerns," he said. He reeled up his rig and carefully swung back toward the bank. Then he gave it a hard side-arm cast toward the river.

The hook, sinker, and bobber went about fifty yards out into the river. The sheephead came off the hook about two thirds of the way through the cast. It flew through the air up the river bank and...you guessed it...hit the old lady right in the side of the head. When it hit, the sheephead knocked her turban down over her eyes and then flopped into the water.

Thunderfoot's mouth dropped open. I looked at the old lady and she was adjusting her turban up onto her head and seemed like she hadn't been hurt, but she was plenty mad. I couldn't keep a straight face and burst out laughing. When I started laughing, Thunderfoot almost tipped over laughing so hard.

Now, I know it wasn't nice to laugh, but there was no way any human, including Thunderfoot could have done that on purpose if he'd have had a year to try. While I felt bad about laughing, it was about one of the funniest things I'd ever seen while fishing.

"I'm gonna go fish downriver," he said taking off down the bank.

"You better go over there and tell her you're sorry," I said.

"No way, her son will kill me."

Just then I had a hard hit on my minnow and set the hook into my fifth walleye. I reeled it in and squatted down to put it on the stringer. As I finished I heard footsteps on the bank behind me. I looked down at my side and there was about a size thirteen tennis shoe. The mate to it was on my other side. Above the tennis shoes were bright blue pants legs of a royal blue jump suit. I knew who was wearing it as I stood up.

The old lady's son was about six foot four and built like William-the-Refrigerator Perry, of Chicago Bears fame a few years back. He looked down at me and glowered.

"You hit my momma up side the *hay-ed* with a fish?"

"No, it wasn't me," I said trying not to let my voice quiver.

"Somebody hit my momma up side the *hay-ed* with a fish."

"Honest, it wasn't me. I saw it happen and I'm sure it was an accident."

He stood there looking down at me. With me standing almost in the water, he was nearly a foot taller than I was. He also had the distinct advantage since my choices were tangle with him or going swimming in an icy river. Neither choice very appetizing.

He stood there thinking about it for what seemed like an eternity and then stomped off up the bank. I turned and saw Thunderfoot downriver from us with tears running down his cheeks from laughing so hard.

"Get up here!" I said as angrily as I could.

He walked back up as slowly as he could go. "You go over there and own up to your stupid move and tell that lady you're sorry."

He walked slowly up the old lady and stopped and gave her one of his famous "charm-smiles". He batted his big blue eyes at her bashfully and I could see that he was telling her hopefully that it was his fault and he was sorry. Soon she beamed and put her arm around his waist and gave him a hug. He began walking back and turned and gave her a wave.

"It's all ok," he said.

He picked up his gear and walked half way up the bank and stopped. "Oh by the way...I told her you would be happy to give her your walleyes for being so careless with your cast." He was off like a shot for the top of the riverbank.

I looked up at the old lady and she was sitting waiting for me with an empty stringer in her hand. That little...he got me again.

Thanks, Thunderfoot.

Luck Is My Middle Name

Thunderfoot and I were climbing slowly up the side of a steep hill on opening morning of his turkey season. Each spring, there are six hunting periods for which a hunter may draw a permit. Thunderfoot had drawn the second period and I had drawn a permit for the fourth season. We always hunted together so it was actually nice that we got different time periods so we could hunt more hours.

We were using the stars for light because the turkeys were roosting just a hundred yards or so up the hill. We didn't dare use a flashlight or make any noise. I bent a branch back and motioned Thunderfoot through the opening as we neared the top of the hill.

"They should be right on that point," I whispered. "Be really quiet or we'll spook them."

Thunderfoot nodded and quietly moved past me. I was amazed that he had been so quiet coming up the hill but we had spent a lot of time in the woods since I had given him his nickname and his stalking skills were much improved.

At the hilltop, I motioned toward a blown-down tree and signaled for him to sit down and wait while I put out our hen decoys. By the time I had the two fake turkeys positioned Thunderfoot had cleared all of the leaves and sticks from our hiding spot. I unfolded a piece of camouflage material and we made a blind by hanging it from the bushes and limbs in front of the treetop.

"This is a cool blind," Thunderfoot whispered. "I think..." Just then a tom turkey cobbled about sixty yards down the hill from us. Thunderfoot's eyes got as big as saucers. "I think we're in the right spot," he said smiling.

Indeed we were and soon another turkey gobbled and then a third sounded off. In a short time there were turkeys gobbling all around us. The ones we were interested in, just down the hill from us were talking up a storm. We waited for about twenty minutes and then heard the toms fly down from the trees. The first one landed very close followed by two more that landed right next to him. "Holy cow!" Thunderfoot whispered. "They're almost in range."

"Just sit still," I said. "They'll see the decoys and come right up here."

Sure enough, one of the toms looked up the hill and saw our decoys. He immediately fanned out his tail and gobbled like crazy. I called back and here he came!

Thunderfoot slid the gun up over the top of the blind and got ready. "Wait for him to get close to the decoy," I said. "It's about fifteen yards away from us, so it'll be an easy shot."

The turkey came closer. Thunderfoot quietly pulled the hammer back on the ten-gauge and took a deep breath. KABOOM!

For about three seconds, the turkey stood there like it was going to drop over. Then it high-tailed it down the side of the hill.

Thunderfoot sat there with his mouth hanging open.

"You missed!" I said. "I can't believe it. How could you miss?" I walked toward the spot where the turkey had been standing. I still could not believe he had missed a bird the size of a medium sized dog with a ten-gauge shotgun. When I turned around I could see his eyes were welling up with tears so I quickly examined a small sapling near where the turkey had been. "Wow, that's the luckiest turkey in this woods," I said. "Most of your shot hit this little tree."

He brightened up at that so I said, "We've got plenty of time. Maybe we can get another one to come into us."

I was actually pretty doubtful about calling in another turkey after we had shot the gun but I wanted to make Thunderfoot feel better. So I gathered up the decoys and we walked to the top of the hill to wait. We ate a couple of candy bars and drank some juice boxes and suddenly a long way off, maybe three hills over, we heard a turkey gobble.

"Listen," Thunderfoot said. "There's one."

We waited and he gobbled again. "Let's move that way," I said. "He's a long way off and we can get away with moving." We took off in the direction of the turkey at a fast walk and stopped partway over the hill. I called on my turkey call and the turkey gobbled right back. This time he was closer to us, so we moved very carefully and called again. When he answered he was just across the valley from us on the other hillside. I couldn't see any way to get any closer to him, so I said, "You sit next to that tree and I'll lay down by this log. We can't move any closer or he'll see us."

Thunderfoot sat down in front of a big oak tree and I lay down behind a log just a few feet from the tree. I called and the turkey gobbled on the hillside right below us. We waited and all of a sudden the turkey materialized out of the brush. He was about fifty yards away....too far for a shot. He was working his way toward us looking for that sweet sounding hen that had been talking to him.

When he disappeared behind a treetop, Thunderfoot raised the gun and got ready. Soon the turkey jumped onto a log about forty yards away. Thunderfoot waited. The turkey hopped down from the log and started up the hill. Thirty-five yards....thirty yards...now he was in range. Twenty-five yards.....on the bird came. Then time stood still for a second.

Thunderfoot touched off the three-and-a-half inch shell and the turkey tipped over like he had been hit by a truck. In the same instant, Thunderfoot was up and on his feet racing down the hill. The turkey flopped around for a couple of seconds, then got to his feet and took off running with Thunderfoot in hot pursuit.

Thunderfoot caught up in a matter of seconds. Since the gun was a single-shot, he grabbed it by the barrel and swung it like a baseball bat, knocking the bird down. Feathers flew as he tossed the gun onto the ground and tackled the turkey.

I sat there dumbfounded watching the whole thing. "Get down here and help me with this thing!" he yelled. Leaves, brush and feathers were flying as the turkey flapped his wings. Thunderfoot was getting a beating from the critter's wings and sharp toenails.

I ran down the hill and picked up a strong stick and cracked the bird over the head. That was the end of that. I sat down and began laughing. "Boy you weren't taking any chances on that one were you?" I said.

"No way! I wasn't going to lose two birds in one day," he said grinning through the dirt and debris that was stuck to the sweat on his face.

We smoothed out the feathers on the turkey and took a couple of pictures. Then we picked up the gun and found Thunderfoot's cap hanging from a tree branch. As we started down the hill I said, "Boy, you've got some luck. Most people get one chance in a whole season for a turkey. Some don't even get that....and you got two chances in one day."

Thunderfoot grinned as he proudly carried his turkey over his shoulder. "Some guys got skill, some got luck...I guess luck is my middle name. Plus, I have the advantage of a pretty good hunting guide."

Maybe so.

Thanks, Thunderfoot.

The Mother Lode

I was sitting on the front patio sipping a soda when Thunderfoot came around the corner of the house carrying a grocery bag. He gave me a grin and held out the bag in front of him. "It looks like a good day to go mushroom hunting," he said.

It was one of those early spring days when the humidity was almost unbearable. There were rain clouds building in the west and I wasn't too excited about tromping up and down the hills looking for mushrooms. With the clouds building up it was a pretty good bet that we'd get caught in a storm anyway. "It's going to rain, and I'm pretty comfortable right here," I said.

"Just think of those big morels popping out of the ground, waiting for us to pick them. Just think of a nice walk in the woods in the spring, communing with nature. Just think..."

"Ok, ok. I give up" I said. There was no use arguing with him and he'd keep pestering me until I gave in, so I decided to just get it over with. I grabbed a plastic bag from the house and off we went for the hills. Thunderfoot wanted to go to one of the farms where we had hunted squirrels last fall. We stopped and ask for permission to hunt and then started off through the woods. We casually walked up the valley and I strolled along the creek and tried to see some brook trout. Thunderfoot, meanwhile, was loping up every hillside along the way, checking out dead trees.

"Any up there?" I asked when he stopped below a tree.

"Just a few, don't bother coming up, I'll get them." He was on his knees picking mushrooms and he didn't have to tell me twice not to climb up the steep hill. Soon he came down and rejoined me. "I got a few," he said opening his mushroom bag and holding it out to me. I looked over the edge of the bag cautiously not knowing what to expect and saw about a dozen nice morels.

"Those aren't bad," I said.

He grinned. "What were you expecting, a snake?"

"I don't trust you after that first time," I said grinning.

He looked offended. "What? Would I do something like that?"

"Yes you would and I'm not going to fall for it twice."

"I'm going way up on top. I remember a big tree up there that was dead from when we were squirrel hunting last fall," he said. "Want to come?"

"Go ahead," I said. "I'll stay down here and look for valley mushrooms."

I sat down next to a shade tree and stretched out. It was nice and cool and the sounds of the stream in the valley soon put me to sleep. I woke about half-an-hour later when something began tickling my nose. I looked up and it was Thunderfoot with a weed in his hand grinning at me.

"Jeez, I could hear you snoring clear up on top of the hill," he said. I was still groggy from sleep but woke fast when he dropped his mushroom sack in my lap. It was full to the top with mushrooms.

"Wow, where did you get those?" I asked.

"Up by that tree I told you about," he said. "And this is only a start. There are about a million more up there."

I was on my feet quickly when he said that and started off to where he had just been when he stopped me. "We need more bags," he said. "These two won't hold all of them."

Now I was really excited. "Honest?" I asked.

"No foolin...we need at least ten bags."

Just then I remembered some shoe bags that were in back of the truck. I had been an usher in a friend's wedding a few weeks earlier and all of the bags and boxes from the other usher's shoes and rented tuxes ended up in a garbage box in the truck. "There are a bunch of those shoe bags in the truck from Jon's wedding," I said. "We can use them."

Thunderfoot was off toward the truck like a shot. I sat down to wait for him even though I could hardly wait for him to get back so I could see this huge mushroom find. I figured I'd better wait since it was his spot, but it didn't take long for him to come huffing and puffing down the valley with an armful of bags.

We headed up the hill, Thunderfoot galloping along at a breakneck pace and me panting along behind him. We got to the top and started down the other side when I saw the tree. It was an enormous elm, probably twenty feet around. The bark was hanging on it just beginning to drop off, a prefect age for a mushroom tree. Thunderfoot stopped in front of the tree, turned and spread his arms like Moses parting the Red Sea. "Behold...the mother lode," he said.

I stood there with my mouth hanging open. I had heard many times of miracle trees where you could find hundreds of mushrooms, but had never found one. This tree was one of those miracle trees. There were mushrooms for thirty feet or forty feet in each direction around the tree. They were so thick in places that you couldn't walk without stepping on them. I stood there taking in the once-in-a-lifetime sight...and then it began to rain.

Thunderfoot and I didn't care if it rained, snowed, or hailed. We both got down on our hands and knees and began crawling around the tree picking mushrooms and filling plastic bags. We picked for over two hours and ran out of bags so Thunderfoot took off his shirt, tied the sleeves and head hole shut and we put the last of the mushrooms in the shirt. We were soaked to the skin, covered in dirt and leaves and we had eleven bags and a t-shirt full of mushrooms. We couldn't have been happier.

We picked up the bags and started back to the truck. "Wow, I've never seen so many mushrooms in one place in my life," I said grinning.

"Just think...you could be still sitting on the porch, nice and dry, and you'd have missed this day," he said.

I looked at my shirtless, wet little buddy and smiled. "I wouldn't have missed this for anything," I said. "And it's even better because I got to share it with you."

He grinned back at me. "This will be one mushroom trip we'll remember for a long time."

No kidding, a long time for sure.

Thanks, Thunderfoot.

Night Fishing

I was just finishing the dishes when I happened to look out my window and saw Thunderfoot coming across the back yard with his arms full of fishing gear. A minute later he came through the front door with a big grin.

"It sure would be a nice night to do some night fishing for catfish," he said with an expectant look on his face. "One of my friends at school went last night and he caught a whole bunch of catfish."

"Fishing at night?" I asked. "You get into enough trouble fishing in the daytime. Don't you think that throwing darkness into the mix will make things a little hazardous?"

He scoffed at me. "I've got a lantern and I already dug worms. All you have to do is grab your pole and we're ready." He nodded his head up and down like a bobble-dead doll.

"Well, I guess it might be fun," I said. "And since you've got everything ready to go, I'll go along."

"Good, I'll load everything up while you make the lunch."

"Lunch?" I had just finished my dinner ten minutes earlier and he was talking about having lunch already? I threw together a few sandwiches and some chips and tossed them into a small cooler with some pop and joined him at the truck.

A little later we walked down the bank of a stream that fed into the river known for a good catfish population. He picked a spot just above a treetop that had fallen into the water. We set up our camp. I got the gear ready while Thunderfoot cut a couple of forked sticks to use as "pole holders."

We had just baited up and tossed out lines out when Thunderfoot opened the cooler saying, "Boy, this fishing makes me faminished, what's in here?" He began inhaling sandwiches and chips as if he'd been without a meal for a week. Suddenly he dropped his food and grabbed his rod and set the hook into a fish. "All right," he said. "That's the first fish of the day, you have to buy ice-cream." He worked the fish close to the bank and slid it up onto the grass. It was a nice sized catfish and he unhooked it, put it on the stringer and re-baited his hook.

Meanwhile I salvaged half of a sandwich from the lunch cooler and settled back in my fishing chair to relax. Actually my fishing chair was really a turkey hunting chair. It was like an aluminum lawn chair but the legs on it were only about six inches long instead of a couple of feet. It was great for turkey hunting because you could sit low where the turkeys wouldn't see you but still have a backrest to lean against. It worked real nice on the river bank for fishing too.

We caught a few more fish and soon darkness began to creep up on us. It was getting hard to see our lines so Thunderfoot lit the lantern and sat it between us on the ground. I was pretty comfortable and getting kind of drowsy when Thunderfoot grabbed his pole and hauled back on it to set the hook. His reel began screaming as the drag was pulled out and his pole was bent nearly double.

"Holy cow! It's a monster!" he yelled. While he fought his fish I was contentedly watching from my chair. I could see that his line was caught in the treetop as the fish had pulled it downriver while fighting him.

"Your fish is under the tree," I said.

"Oh yeah? I've got strong line on here, I'll winch him right out of there," he said as he hauled back on his pole. I started to sit up to get a better look just as his line came clear of the tree. His "fish" came out of the water and flew through the air right at me. Now, it was pretty dark and it all happened pretty fast, but what I saw flying through the air was a long snake-like critter coming right at me. It landed in my lap and began writhing around as I tipped my chair over backwards. I was skidding backwards and got turned toward the river and in less than a second I rolled off the bank into the water with the snake-thing in my lap.

I may have set a world record for the backstroke from a sitting position because it only took a couple of seconds to get out into the middle of the river. Meanwhile, Thunderfoot had reeled up the slack in his line. He began to pull the snake-thing and me toward the bank. The critter was wrapped around one of my chair arms. After a couple of pulls it came free. He pulled it up onto the bank while I floundered around in the water.

"Hey, it's an eel!" he said cheerfully. "Come here and look at it...it's cool."

I was standing in chest deep water, my fishing chair floating around next to me and he wanted me to look at his eel. I stood there and let my heart rate slow down to less than three hundred beats per minute and then slogged my way to the riverbank dragging my chair behind me. The eel was writhing around on the ground and Thunderfoot was standing there looking at it with the lantern in his hand.

He looked up at me. "Will you take it off? It's kind of creepy and I don't want to touch it."

When he saw the look on my face he said, "Oh never mind, I'll just cut the line."

He clipped the line a little way from the critter and it slithered down over the bank and back into the river. It was probably going to look for a new place to call home.

I was standing there dripping wet, covered in stinky mud and still panting when Thunderfoot said, "Boy, you sure can move fast when you want to. I never saw anybody jump so high from a sitting position." He was smirking as he looked me up and down.

"Thanks for noticing. And, by the way, no I'm not hurt."

"I knew you weren't hurt, you moved too fast to be hurt," he said. "I suppose you want to go home now. We might as well. You probably scared all the fish away when you went swimming anyway."

Sometimes he was such a compassionate boy.

Thanks, Thunderfoot.

The Fish Fry

Thunderfoot came through my front door carrying his fishing pole and a sleeping bag. "What'cha doin' tonight?" he asked.

"I don't have anything planned. What do you have in mind?"

"It's such a nice evening. I think we should go set up the tent on a sandbar and fish late, and then sleep overnight on the sandbar. Sounds good huh?"

I didn't really have anything better to do so I agreed. We began gathering gear that we would need for the evening. We put the small tent, our sleeping bags, a couple of rods and reels and a lantern in the boat plus a cooler and some pop.

"We'll have to stop at the grocery store and get some hot dogs or brats for supper," I said.

"No way...we'll eat fish. Let's just take some potatoes and beans and bread. We'll catch some fish, clean them and fry them up. It'll be great."

"Maybe we should take some hot dogs, just in case," I said.

"Are you in doubt of my ability to procure food for myself and my fellow explorer? No way. No hot dogs and no brats will be taken. We will eat fish." His mind was made up.

A short time later we were cruising down the river. My dog Sophie stood in the bow as we drove along looking for a good sandbar to set up our camp. We hadn't gone too far when Thunderfoot began pointing to the right and declared that we had found the perfect spot.

It did look like a good fishing spot, with a nice current break just below the bar and a high, dry sandbar for camping. We pulled the boat up on the dry sand and began setting up our little camp. I was working on the tent when I heard a splash and looked to see Thunderfoot and Sophie in the river goofing around as only kids and dogs can. In a few minutes I had everything ready and Thunderfoot ran back dripping wet with Sophie right on his heels.

"Just remember, when we go to bed, Sophie is sleeping on your side of the tent," I said at which he grinned from ear to ear. He and Sophie were good buddies and he didn't care if she smelled a little like wet dog.

"Let's fish," he said. "I'm getting hungry."

We baited up and cast out our lines and sat back on the edge of the sandbar with our feet in the water to wait for a bite. Sophie watched expectantly. We waited. And we waited. And we waited some more. Finally Thunderfoot got a bite and when he set the hook he missed the fish.

"Nice going," I said. "Looks like I'll have to catch enough for both of us."

A minute later I got a bite and set the hook into a good-sized fish. I fought it to the sandbar and when it got close I could see it was a carp.

"Let's see you eat that," Thunderfoot said chuckling.

I let the carp go and we continued fishing for another hour. "Wow, it's getting pretty late and we still don't have any supper," he said looking pitiful. "Maybe you should take the boat back and get some hot dogs after all."

"Oh year, sure," I said. "I wanted to bring some just in case but oh no, you wouldn't hear of it. Now its pitch dark out and you want me to go up the river and get some weenies. Well, I hope you like fried potatoes and beans because that's what we're going to have for supper."

"Well, you don't have to be nasty about it," he said acting hurt. Then he grinned. "Beans are my favorite fruit anyway."

After another forty-five minutes of fishing we could see that our fish fry was going to be fishless, so I set my pole down and began lighting the stove. I peeled potatoes and chopped them up with some onions and put them on the fire in a frying pan. Thunderfoot kept fishing while the food cooked. I put the beans into a pot, set them on the stove and when everything was ready he reluctantly came over and sat down in the sand to eat. He scooped a big spoonful of beans onto a slice of bread and made a bean sandwich.

"I'll just pretend it's a walleye fillet," he said as he chomped down on his food.

We ate the whole pan of potatoes and beans except for the portion we gave Sophie and mopped up all of the bread with the other food.

"Boy, I'm stuffed," Thunderfoot said. "That wasn't so bad after all."

I had begun cleaning up the supper mess and Sophie was busy licking every molecule of food from her dish when Thunderfoot sprang to his feet and ran to his pole. He grabbed it and began fighting a fish that seemed to be a good size. Finally he lifted a nice walleye from the water. "Wow, look at this," he said.

Just then my pole began jumping with a bite and I too had a good walleye. I took it off the hook and put it back into the river.

"What did you do that for?" he asked.

"We already ate. We might as well put them back. We don't have enough ice to keep them until morning."

He grudgingly released his fish and we both re-baited and cast back out. Within a minute we each were fighting another fish. This time I had a bass and he had a nice catfish. We released them. A few minutes later we were fighting more fish and the action continued until we ran out of worms.

"Wow, I don't think we've ever caught fish that fast before," he said as he reeled in for the last time. We put our poles away and crawled into the tent. We wiped off our feet and crawled in with Sophie coming in right behind us. Sophie snuggled down by Thunderfoot and things began to quiet down. I was lying there listening to the night sounds and the sound of Sophie snoring when Thunderfoot whispered. "You asleep yet?"

"No."

"This is cool, huh?"

"Yeah, it's good."

After a few minutes of silence he said, "I think supper was good even without fish."

"It was ok," I said sleepily.

"It was good. But next time you shouldn't listen to a kid. You're the grown-up, you should be the one to decide to bring hot dogs or not."

"I'll remember that."

Thanks, Thunderfoot.

Just Call Me Humphrey Bogart

"We really need a blind on the grassy puddle," Thunderfoot said as he searched my refrigerator for something to snack on. "That's the best pond in the swamp. If we had a blind there we would get more ducks and be a lot more comfortable."

I was in agreement but the grassy puddle, as we called it, was a long way from the high bank where we parked the truck. That meant it was a long way to carry all the materials that it took to build a duck blind. The distance was close to half-a-mile each way, and the trail was through head tall grass. "We'd be better off to wait until winter and then slide everything out there on some sleds," I said. I was hoping to escape the torture of hauling lumber and chicken wire to the pond in extremely hot weather that we were now experiencing. I might as well have saved my breath because Thunderfoot was already making work details for our first night of labor.

"If we build the floor here and then haul it down there and carry it out in one trip it will save a lot of walking," he said. Then we go back to the truck for the posts for the corners and it only takes two trips. We'll have the worst part done. I've got some lumber and posts. Should we go now, or wait until after supper. By the way, what's for supper?"

An hour and a half and a dozen brats later we were nailing the boards together for the floor. Of course by the time we finished, it had become a lot bigger and heavier than we had anticipated. It was all Thunderfoot and I could do to get it into the back of the pickup, let alone carry it across the swamp.

"I'll call Scot," he said. "He'll help us, and he's pretty strong." In a few minutes Scot, one of Thunderfoot's friends from school, arrived in a great cloud of dust sliding his bike to a halt in the driveway. Since he often hunted with us he was more than willing to help. "Let's go," Thunderfoot said, and we headed toward the duck marsh.

We hauled the floor down over the high bank and started out across the swamp. It was tough going and of course, they let me lead, breaking the trail. The grass was shoulder high and the footing was mushy at best and soupy at worst. Much of the tall grass was cut-grass and it soon slashed my arms and face into a bloody pulp. After about two hundred yards of work I called for a breather. I was about to have a coronary and Thunderfoot and Scot were barely breathing hard.

"You know, we should get this thing out there before duck season opens, and it's only a month away," Thunderfoot said. I glared at him, wiped the sweat from my eyes and picked up my end of the floor.

After two more stops we were at the edge of the pond. I was gasping for breath so I sat down on the blind floor to rest while the boys ran back to the truck for the posts and the sledge hammer. They returned much too soon. When I started to get up I got a cramp in my left calf. As I tried to straighten it out the right one cramped up too. I let out a yell and keeled over into the grass, thrashing around like I had some kind of voodoo curse.

Thunderfoot just stood there with his mouth open looking at me. Scot looked like he was ready to run for the hills, not wanting to be around when I expired. I was in agony, wallowing around in the mud, cramped up like a pretzel.

The cramps finally relaxed and I straightened out my legs. I struggled to my feet and the boys still hadn't said a word. They both just stood there with amazed looks on their faces.

"Are you going to die or what?" Thunderfoot finally asked.

"If I have to go through a double cramp like that again, I'd rather die," I said.

"Well, let's get this done before you do," he said. He handed me the mall and a post. I waded out to waist-deep water and began pounding the post into the mud. It went easily for about two feet. Then it hit hard bottom and it took a lot more energy to get it any deeper. After a few minutes, the post was solid. We measured the position for the second post and the third and forth and I pounded them into the mud.

"They're not the same height," Thunderfoot said looking critically at my work.

"The small chain saw is in the truck," I said. "Go back and get it and we'll have to even them up with that." They both took off sprinting for the truck and I had a breather standing in the cool water.

When they arrived with the chain saw I measured and marked each of the posts and then began cutting them off. Thunderfoot was impressed with my work when I finished and had a satisfied look on his face. "Not bad," he said.

He and Scot went back for the floor which would sit right on top of the posts if we had everything measured correctly. Soon I saw them struggling through the marsh toward me. When they were just a short way away from me, I saw Thunderfoot look down into the water and a look of horror came over his face. Scot's eyes followed his and he let out a yell and released his end of the floor and ran for high ground.

I didn't want to look down but I had to. I saw about two hundred leeches swimming around my legs in the water. "Hurry up with that floor," I said. "Get it over here, so I can get it up on the posts and get out of the water."

Thunderfoot slid the floor over to me and took off for the bank. I man-handled it up onto the posts and it fit perfectly. Then I crawled up onto it and turned down my hip boots that were full of water since the water was deeper than the boots were tall. A gush of water and leeches poured out onto the floor.

"Are any stuck on you?" Thunderfoot asked.

"I don't think so," I said inspecting my legs and feet. Then I got a funny feeling just inside the leg of my shorts. I lifted up the material to find a leech hooked onto my thigh very close to my parts that seldom see sunlight.

"Oh no! He's hooked on you. Oh, yuck!" Thunderfoot grimaced. He was about as fond of leeches as I was of snakes.

I took hold of the leech and pulled steadily until it let loose of my leg and then tossed it into the water. There was a small spot that bled but he apparently hadn't been hooked onto me long enough to do much damage.

Thunderfoot threw me a hammer and bag of nails and I nailed down the floor. Then I waded back to the higher ground.

"That was *gross,*" he said. "You know what were gonna build out here next?"

"No, what are we going to build?"

"A bridge."

Thanks, Thunderfoot.

The Opener

"Well, what did he say?" Thunderfoot asked as he burst through my front door on a dead run.

"What did who say?" I answered trying to act dumb.

He gave me one of his exasperated looks. "Ken! What did Ken say?"

"Oh Ken. I didn't know what you were talking about. Well, I called him and we talked a while about you and I hunting on the old farm. We talked about the price of milk and...."

"If you're trying to make me crazy, you're doing a good job," he interrupted. "What did he say about us hunting there?"

I grinned. "He said yes. We can hunt on the old farm and we'll have it all to ourselves."

Thunderfoot jumped into the air and let out a yell. "All-righty-then!"

The previous spring we had hunted on this farm for turkeys and we loved the place. It was a small farm but had a lot of good hunting ground on it and we had gotten to know our way around pretty well. The best part was that we'd be the only ones hunting there, so we would be safe and not have to worry about others getting in our way. During the turkey season we'd seen a lot of deer on the farm, so we decided to ask permission to hunt deer there in the upcoming season. Now we had permission to do just that.

"Wow, this is so cool," Thunderfoot said. "We need to go up there and scout it out, so we can find a good place to sit. And we need to get some stuff up there to sit on and some stuff for shelter if it rains and some food together and..."

"Whoa," I said. "Deer season is a month off. We don't need to start making sandwiches just yet."

He looked up and grinned. "Yeah, I guess we can wait a while to make the lunch."

Over the next coupe of weeks we went up to the farm several

times. We just sat and watched the deer, turkeys, squirrels, and foxes that made the place their home. We watched where the deer came from and where they went. Soon we had a pretty good idea of where to sit on opening day.

Thunderfoot dragged more and more gear over to my house each day and soon my porch began to look like a garage sale was in progress. We had two of almost everything that had ever been invented for deer hunting and three of some of the essential items that Thunderfoot felt were more important. He wasn't leaving anything to chance.

Thunderfoot and I each carried gear up the hill three times the day before the season opened. We had stools to sit on, plastic for rain protection, binoculars, cushions, hand warmers, knives, ropes, and an assortment of candy bars and snacks. I had chosen a corner in a field that looked over the entire hilltop. Thunderfoot was going to sit at the top of an old road that came up the hill just across the field from where I was sitting.

Thunderfoot nearly ran up the hill with each load while I struggled along, sweating and panting, waiting for my heart to explode in my chest. When we finally got everything up the hill we were ready for anything Mother Nature could throw at us.

That night Thunderfoot slept at my house. Well he mostly paced around in the dark most of the night. I got a good night's sleep until 4:30 a.m. when Thunderfoot turned my bedroom light on and reminded me that it was time to get ready. I made bacon and eggs but he was too nervous to eat. So I cleaned up the dishes and we took off into the dark morning. We had about a ten minute drive and it was over an hour and a half until shooting time.

Thunderfoot was ready to go when we got to the farm. "Why don't we wait a half hour or so?" I asked. "Otherwise we'll be cold by daylight."

He would have nothing to do with that suggestion and took off up to his stand. I slid back in the seat, closed my eyes and woke back up about a half hour before opening time. I walked leisurely up the hill to my stand just as the black sky was turning into a deep blue. Stumps and clumps of grass that had looked like deer or other critters standing along the way soon became what they really were as the light increased. I sat in my chair and nestled down and got comfortable. A short time later, I heard shooting in the distance. The season was open.

I noticed some movement off to my right and watched as two hen turkeys came into the field and began to feed. I was enjoying them when one of the hens suddenly looked up and clucked. I looked across the field in the direction she was looking and saw three does moving across the pasture. They were headed right for Thunderfoot, so I didn't move. Soon they were gone and no sound came from his stand. I figured he didn't see them or let them go.

The sun came up over the hill and I got real relaxed, closing my eyes for just a second. Suddenly I felt something on my nose and awoke with a jolt to find Thunderfoot standing there with a weed in his hand that he had been tickling my nose with.

"Have a nice nap?" he asked grinning.

"I wasn't sleeping. I was just resting my eyes."

"It's ten o'clock...that was a long blink."

Ten o'clock! I had been sleeping for three hours.

"I could hear you snoring all the way down the hill. By the way, do you have anything left to eat?"

"I have all of my lunch left. What happened to yours?"

"It's been gone for a long time," he said as he dug through my food pack.

"Did you see those does?" I asked.

"Yeah, but I'm shooting a buck," he said helping himself to one of my ham sandwiches. He took a huge bite and said mumbling, "Boy, I was starting to get cold." His eyes suddenly got as big as silver dollars. He tried to swallow the big chunk of ham but he began gasping for air. He pointed frantically across the field. I looked where he was pointing and saw two bucks and a doe heading right for us.

"Get down on one knee," I said quietly. "Let them keep coming."

He knelt down chewing furiously trying to get the ham swallowed. The buck on the left was much larger than the one on the right. The doe was right between them and they were still coming right at us with no idea we were there. "When they get close, you shoot the one on the left and I'll take the one on the right. Ok?"

Thunderfoot nodded and gripped his gun so tightly his knuckles were white. "Just stay calm and shoot when you're ready," I advised. "It's just like target shooting."

The deer came on, unhurried and suddenly Thunderfoot touched off a shot. The deer all jumped up and began running in different directions and soon everything was mass confusion. I'll never know who shot what, but when the smoke cleared the smaller buck lay in the field and the doe and larger buck had disappeared into the woods. Thunderfoot was up and running toward the downed deer. I picked up my knife and followed him.

When I got there I could see how excited he was. He put his hand on the deer's side and petted it a little and had a sad look in his eyes. "We got him."

I nodded.

"Did you shoot him, or did I?" he asked.

"You got this one. I was shooting at the other one."

His response was a grin.

"He sure is pretty," he said quietly.

"Are you ok?" I asked.

"Yeah, I'm ok. It's kind of funny though isn't it? I'm glad I got him but I'm kinda sad I killed him too. Is that stupid?"

I squatted down and put my arm around his shoulder. "That's not stupid at all. In fact I'm glad you feel that way. It shows you have respect for his life. Hunting is mostly getting ready and waiting. The killing part is the smallest part of it, but it's necessary. It's just life."

He nodded thoughtfully.

"Well, now the fun starts. Do you think you can field dress him?"

"No problem," he said. He took the knife out of the sheath and we turned the deer over. He put the knife to the belly, just below the ribs and paused. He looked up at me. "Maybe you could show me."

I smiled and thought back to the first time I'd dressed a deer and how scared I was of messing up. "No problem," I said.

Thanks, Thunderfoot.

The Gift of the Munchkin

"What're you doin' with that barrel?" Thunderfoot asked as he came around the corner of the house.

"It's a nail keg. I got it at the lumber yard. I'm going to cut a piece of plywood to cover the open end and then cut a hole in and it will be a squirrel house."

I began tracing the keg on an old scrap of plywood and Thunderfoot stood there with his mouth hanging open watching me. I got out my jigsaw and began cutting out the circle of plywood.

"You're making a squirrel house?" he asked. "What in the world are you making a squirrel house for?"

"Why not? I answered. "Squirrels need someplace to live too." I began cutting a hole in the plywood circle for a doorway and Thunderfoot held the piece steady for me as I cut.

In a few minutes I had the plywood nailed onto the front of the keg and went to the shed for a ladder. "I'm glad you showed up," I said. "You can climb up the tree and nail this up for me. You wouldn't want an old man to fall out of a tree and hurt himself would you?"

He just grinned at me and grabbed the keg, put a few nails in his pocket and climbed the ladder. I tossed the hammer up to him and he nailed the squirrel house between a branch and the main trunk of the tree. As he came down the ladder he just shook his head. "I always figured you were getting a little off in the head, but now I'm sure of it. You do remember we go hunting for squirrels don't you? Now you're making little homes for them?"

"The ones we hunt are country squirrels. These are town squirrels. Besides I like to watch them at the bird feeders. If I make them a house they'll have a nice place to sleep after they eat all my birdseed."

I put the ladder away and suggested that we go out to a friend's farm and do a little rabbit hunting. I didn't have to persuade Thunderfoot. He ran home and got his gun while I changed into my hunting clothes. Twenty minutes later we were in the woods hunting bunnies.

When we came to the biggest, thickest hill on the farm, I took the path around the bottom while Thunderfoot headed up to the top of the hill. I was walking along slowly when a rabbit took off up the hill. From where I was I couldn't get a shot but soon I heard a shot from Thunderfoot. A couple of seconds later there was another shot and then another. From the sound of things that rabbit was probably pretty safe.

We worked around the hill and Thunderfoot shot another three times. I saw one more rabbit off in the distance but didn't get a shot. I sat down to rest on a log and it wasn't long before I awoke with a "where in the world am I" feeling. I looked around and then realized where I was. I heard a snicker from behind me.

"Jeez, I could hear you snoring clear back at the truck."

"I just closed my eyes for a second," I said.

"More like half an hour," he said laughing.

I was still confused as I got up to go back to the truck. "Any bunnies?" I asked.

He shook his head.

Our farmer friend was in the yard and came over to visit with us. He winked at Thunderfoot as we got into the truck.

"What was that wink about?" I asked.

"Oh, I did a little business while you were getting your beauty sleep."

"What business?"

"None of yours."

A week later Thunderfoot came through the door with a big feed sack under his arm. "Got any squirrels yet?"

"Yeah, I think so," I said. "I think two of them are living in the barrel. I've seen them go in and out several times."

"Cool."

"What's in the sack?" I asked.

"You're not going to say I'm a sissy are you?"

"What do you mean?"

"I don't want you to think I'm getting soft. Last week when we were rabbit hunting I asked our friend if I could buy a sack of ear corn to feed the squirrels. So I did and this is it."

"Why would I think you're getting soft?

"Because I hunt squirrels and now I'm feeding them too."

I smiled at him. "Why do you want to feed them?"

"Well, we're not going to shoot these town squirrels and they're kind of cool to watch, so I guess it couldn't hurt to give them a little Christmas present. I think they might like it."

I put my arm around his shoulder and said, "You know, all the hours I've spent teaching you about hunting and fishing have been well spent. A lot of people go their whole lives thinking about killing and taking all they can get, and never think about giving back. You've learned a lot more than I thought."

"Well, I guess I've learned that there's more to hunting and fishing than a full game bag. Just being there matters a lot more than a full bag limit," he said smiling. "And the Lord knows, we don't often have a full bag limit."

"Let's go out and put a nail in that tree and stick an ear of corn on it," I said.

We walked out and made a simple squirrel feeder and then went back into the house to watch. It wasn't long before the two squirrels came sneaking down the tree and began checking the corn out. They sat down on either side of the corn and began eating. We watched for a while and then they got up and scampered up the tree into the squirrel house.

"Merry Christmas to you Mr. and Mrs. Squirrel," Thunderfoot said.

And to you too, friend.

Thanks, Thunderfoot.

One Will Do Nicely

I had called one of my friends who lives near the Mississippi River and he assured me that the ice was thick enough on the river for ice-fishing. Thunderfoot and I didn't have to think twice about that and we were now heading for our fist trip of the year on the ice. We usually stuck closer to home since we had a lot of good fishing spots within a mile of the house, but Thunderfoot had been wanting to try the "Big River" for a quite a while so here we were on our way.

"I didn't see any lunch in the pails," he said looking worried. "Are we going to stop for groceries?"

I smiled. "Nope, we're going to take a break at lunch time and go in for a burger."

He looked at me. "One burger? You know how hungry fishing makes me don't you?"

I just grinned at him. "One will be enough...trust me."

The conversation was soon over because I was pulling alongside a bunch of cars parked near a makeshift parking area along the railroad tracks that ran along the riverbank. Thunderfoot leaped out and began unloading fishing gear and piling it onto our sled. "Oh boy, let's get going. This looks really good."

He started down the steep bank and I followed along at a slower, safer pace. He was already on the ice when I got to the edge and he stopped and looked back at me. "Look at this! There are hundreds of fish down there!"

I caught up to him and as we walked we could see hundreds of bluegills swimming away from us. Every time one of us took a step they swam off in schools like flocks of birds. "Holy cow! Let's get some holes drilled!" he said over his shoulder as he approached a group of fishermen. I had been watching the fishermen on the way out and not one of them had pulled a fish up, so I moved off a little way away from them and set up my fishing area. As I walked I could see fish moving ahead of me in amazing numbers. Any time someone on the ice walked around, the fish scattered. I began to have a feeling that things weren't going to be as good as we hoped they would be.

After about an hour of fishing I walked over to Thunderfoot and he looked up glumly. "They're not going to bite, are they?"

I shook my head. "They're too spooked by the clear ice. I'm afraid we're wasting our time." He looked miserable. "Let's go get a burger and decide what to do next."

He brightened up when he heard that. After hunting and fishing, eating was his favorite pastime. We drove downriver to the next small town and went into a bar and grill. We sat at a table and a waitress came over to take our order. "I'm pretty hungry," Thunderfoot said. "Maybe I'll have a couple burgers."

She looked him up and down and then looked at me and grinned. "First time here?" she asked and I nodded. Then to Thunderfoot she said, "You better start with one. If you finish that one, we'll make you another." Then she walked away.

Thunderfoot looked at me with an amazed look. "Boy, she's got a lot of nerve. Apparently she doesn't have any idea of the capacity I have for burgers." I just shrugged my shoulders.

About twenty minutes later, just as Thunderfoot was about to collapse from hunger, the waitress came with our food. She set the little plastic baskets holding our burgers and fries in front of us and watched as Thunderfoot's eyes bugged out. "Stricken" was about the only way you could describe his slack-jawed expression as he stared at the biggest burger he'd ever seen. "Holy smokes, how many cows do you go through in a week?" She walked off chuckling.

This particular bar was known far and wide for these huge burgers. Each burger starts out in the neighborhood of three quarters of a pound of meat. Then cheese and onions are added and the thing is way more than most people can eat. Thunderfoot looked the monster burger over for a while and then decided to attack it. He gnawed away at the thing and shoveled fries into his mouth and had just about conquered the thing when he looked up. "I don't know if I can finish this. Hey look...it's snowing."

I looked out the window and it was snowing like crazy. It was a typical late spring snow storm that would cover the ground and then be melted in a few hours. Suddenly both Thunderfoot and I looked at each other with the same thought. The ice was now covered with snow. The spooky bluegills wouldn't be able to see us. We finished up as fast as we could and headed back up to the fishing spot.

As we walked down toward the other fishermen I could see them all catching fish one after the other. There were fish flopping all over the ice and we sat down at a couple of holes that were not being used and began fishing.

For the next hour, we caught fish so fast that we didn't have time to keep track of them. Finally as much as I hated to do it, I stopped and counted up the fish we had on the ice. "We've got to see how many we have," I said. "I don't want to go over the limit."

"You count...I'll fish," Thunderfoot said. This was his usual solution to the number-of-fish problem. I began counting and putting the fish into a bucket as I counted them. In no time one bucket was filled and the other soon was also full. "We've got enough," I said. I slid six flopping fish back into the water since they were over our limit.

"No way. You want to quit when they're biting like this?"

"I don't want to quit but we can't take any more."

He looked crushed. We gathered up our gear and loaded up the sled. "I've never caught fish in the ice so fast," he said. "This is the best fishing day I've ever had."

When we got back to the truck we loaded up and started down the road. We were just coming into the town with the big burgers and I looked over at Thunderfoot. "Ready for another burger yet?"

"I think I'll wait a week or so before I eat again. One of those will do quite nicely," he said.

I couldn't believe it...Thunderfoot was filled up.

Not quite.

"I probably could force down an ice-cream cone if we happened to go past an ice-cream store," he said. "You know, ice-cream melts down in all the little cracks where there's room in your stomach, so there's always room for ice-cream."

That's my boy.

Thanks, Thunderfoot.

It'll be Cheaper, and Better

"I think we need one of these," Thunderfoot proclaimed pointing to a new ice shanty that was displayed in a big-box store we were browsing through. "This is really nice, and that thing we're fishing in is about done for."

I had to admit he was right. My old ice shanty had seen better days. There were patches on the patches on the old one and it was pretty well ready for the dump. But the price on these new ones was a little more than I felt like spending right then, so I said, "That would be nice, but look at the price."

He looked at the tag and nodded his head. "Yea it is pretty pricey...hey, why don't I build us a new one? I've got wood and all we need is some pipes and some cloth and bingo, we've got a new shanty. It'll be cheaper and better than this thing."

For some reason I wasn't quite as enthusiastic as he was. I remembered back to his duck blind project that turned out the size of a garage and nearly drowned me when we tried to get it to the marsh. "I don't know, you usually get carried away on these projects."

He gave me one of those looks. "Trust me," he said.

We went home and I kind of forgot about the whole thing when three days later the phone rang. It was Thunderfoot. "Is it ok if I charge a few things at the hardware store on your account?"

"Charge what?" I asked. "What are you building now?"

"The shanty...I need some stuff like connectors and a few nails and staples and stuff," he said.

"Oh," I said. "I didn't know you were actually doing that project. I guess its ok for you to get some stuff, just tell them I said it was all right."

Big mistake.

The weekend was at hand and Thunderfoot came stomping up my front steps early on Saturday morning. "Well are you ready to give the shanty a try?" he asked.

"You actually finished it?"

He gave me a disgusted look. "Of course I finished it…and it's a beauty."

I was skeptical, but I got my boots on and we walked over to his garage to see the new shanty. When he opened the garage door I just stood there with my mouth hanging open. This thing wasn't an ice-shanty it was the size of a small shed. It must have measured nearly eight feet on a side and was at least seven feet tall. It was made out of plywood, conduit and orange sailcloth.

"We'll have a lot more room in this one," he said nodding his head up and down.

"How are we going to get it onto the ice?"

He strode over to the shanty and tugged at one corner. A seam that was held together with Velcro opened up. We crawled through the opening and inside the frame consisted of conduit pipes and connectors. These connectors were screwed down to a plywood floor with a one-by-seven-foot-wide hole cut in one half. This was obviously the place we'd fish through. There was a seam in the middle of the floor that was hinged so it could be folded in half.

"It's simple," Thunderfoot said. "You just take these little connectors out of these little holes and they all come apart. The pipes go on the floor and the cloth comes down and the whole thing folds in the middle with all the parts inside. Then we just latch it together and pull it with this handy rope I've attached to the end."

He took the thing down and it all packed nicely into the floor, which when folded up looked like a very thin casket. "For easy maneuvering, I've installed skis on the half that will stay on the ice."

I had to admit I was pretty impressed. "I've got to admit, you did a good job on it," I said. "How heavy is it?"

He got a worried look on his face. "Well, it got a little out of hand in the weight department. I think we can pull it pretty easy, especially when we get it on slick ice."

I went home and got the truck so we could take the shanty for a "test drive" as Thunderfoot said. I backed up to the door and we grabbed the shanty to lift it into the truck. We could hardly budge the thing. "A little heavy? This weighs a ton!" I said.

"Oh quit acting like a wuss and lift," he grumbled.

We finally managed to get the shanty into the truck and took off for the lake. I backed as close to the ice as I could get and we slid the shanty off onto the ground. It slid along pretty well as long as we were on a packed trail but when we set out across the lake in the deep snow we could barely move it.

"Oh yeah, this is lots better than one of those other shanties," I said grunting.

"Oh dry up and pull!" he said glaring at me.

We finally made it to a good fishing area and Thunderfoot began his assembly while I drilled holes. After much clattering and cussing the shanty was finally up and looked pretty good. I opened the corner where the door was and stepped inside. It was pretty cozy in there and there was a lot of room for gear and people.

"See? I told you this was going to be good," he said proudly surveying his creation. We got our poles out and fished for a couple of hours. The shanty was really comfortable and roomy. As the sun began to set we took the shanty down and began dragging it back to the truck. I nearly had the *Big One* pulling the thing up the high bank to the parking lot.

As we got into town I said, "I'll stop and pay the bill at the hardware store as long as we're going past it."

"Oh, why don't you wait...they're in no hurry. I'm sure they trust you."

"Well, I might as well get it over with," I said as I pulled into the front of the store and parked.

"You coming in?" I asked.

"No I'm pretty tired I think I'll just wait here."

I went in and talked to my friend who owned the store and

then asked for the bill. He picked up a pile of receipts and totaled them up on the adding machine. "It comes to "$237.56," he said.

I almost fainted. "Are you sure those are all mine" I asked.

"Yeah, they're from some project your neighbor kid said you were doing."

When I got back to the truck Thunderfoot was pretending to sleep.

"Do you know how much you spent for this shanty that would save me a lot of money? I asked.

He didn't move. "I said," I repeated.

"I heard you the first time," he said opening one eye. "I'm not sure but I think I went a bit over budget."

"A bit over budget? We could have bought the one in the store and had money left over to buy bait all winter."

"Well, I might have overdone it a bit but look at how nice this shanty is. Other than being a bit heavy, it'll be a great place for us to fish all winter. And think of the bonding we can do."

I laughed. "Yeah we'll bond all right. Maybe we can have a barn dance in it to help pay for it."

We backed out and started down the street. Thunderfoot hemmed and hawed and finally said, "I hesitate to bring this up, but there is one teeny little other bill that needs to be paid.'

"What bill?"

"Well I couldn't sew the cloth myself, so I took it to that upholsterer guy on the corner. He did all the sewing for only $25. Good deal huh?"

Good deal for you maybe.

Thanks, Thunderfoot.

The Polar Expedition

"I just got a call from my buddy on the Mississippi," I said as Thunderfoot answered the phone. "The ice is breaking up today and should be gone by morning."

"What time are we leaving?" he asked without hesitation.

"I'll pick you up at six...be ready."

It was early spring and this would be our first trip to the Mississippi for walleyes. The ice below the dams didn't get as thick as the rest of the river and consequently it went out much earlier in the spring. My friend lived just a short way from the dam and kept an eye on it for me and had called when the ice began breaking up.

Ice-out-day is often one of those once-in-a-season days. The fish have been congregating below the ice at the dams all winter waiting for spawning time to arrive. They are hungry and have seen few fishermen for quite a long time, so when the ice goes out, the first fishermen at the dam can usually have some amazingly good fishing. Thunderfoot and I were going to be some of those chosen ones this spring.

The next morning he started loading his gear into the truck before I was even ready. Soon he was waiting and trying to hurry me. "All you gotta do is back up to the boat and I'll hook it on," he said. In no time we were coming down the river side of the Mississippi bluffs and pulling into the boat landing. "The ice isn't all gone yet, but the other boats have made a pretty good channel through it," I said surveying the river. The landing was about a mile downriver from the dam and much of the broken up ice was being held in place by an island that plugged the channel in the spring. The earlier boats had maneuvered their way through the floating chunks and we were going to do the same thing.

Thunderfoot was in the bow directing me. "Whoa...go right. Whoa...more right. OK, now straight...whoa more right again." It

111

took us about ten minutes to get through the ice and then we headed up to the dam. As we coasted to a stop Thunderfoot had his rod ready and as soon as we stopped he dropped his jig to the bottom. He only lifted it twice when he set the hook into a walleye.

"Yahoo! This is just like in the movies," he said grinning as he reeled the fish up. "By the way, you have the honor of buying me an ice cream on the way home." He was grinning.

I got my rod out and soon was fighting a walleye too. "Boy this is the way it should be all the time," I said. I released the small fish and said, "Let's not keep too many right away. If we get greedy we'll have to quit too soon."

We had an absolute ball for the next two hours. We caught walleyes and sauger about as fast as we could reel tem up. "This is the best fish...wow, look at the ice," Thunderfoot said.

I turned around and looked. The channel we had used to come upriver was now gone. Boat traffic and wind had plugged it up tight with huge blocks of ice.

"Oh-oh. We're gonna have some fun getting back," Thunderfoot said. Then as if it were a sign from above it started snowing. Well, snowing isn't probably the best word... blizzard, or maybe white-out would be better. In a matter of minutes the boat was inches deep with heavy snow. We couldn't see for more than a few feet in any direction.

"I think we better start back," I said.

"What? Are you serious? The fish are biting like mad, and you want to leave?"

"I don't want to leave, but if it keeps snowing like this we're going to have a hard time getting home with the boat behind us. A few more minutes and then we better start back."

In ten minutes it was snowing even harder and things were going from bad to worse. We put our rods away and Thunderfoot got in the bow of the boat. We began working our way downriver through the ice blocks. There were about a dozen other boats with us so we weren't alone. It was slow going and often we had to stop and look over the side to see which way the current was going so we knew which way to go. The snow was so thick that we couldn't see the bank so we had no idea where we were. Finally we got the idea of running the bow of the boat up on the chunks and then we both walked to the bow and the boat broke through. Then we'd repeat that action. It worked pretty well and soon all the other boats were following us like little ducks through the blizzard.

"I'm going to work us to the left so we can see the bank," I said. "Otherwise we'll miss the boat landing."

We angled to our left and many icebergs later the boat landing came into view. We beached the boat and I walked up to the parking lot and got the truck. I backed the truck down and we managed to get the boat loaded. We were strapping the boat down and Thunderfoot said, "Boy this is one fishing trip we'll remember for a while."

I was sure he was right. A short time later we were creeping down the highway toward home. "At this rate it'll take s two hours to get home," I said.

"Yeah but the fishing was worth it. And the ice jam and all the snow, that was a good adventure," he said grinning. "It was like a polar expedition...but you know..."

I looked at my fishing buddy. He had dropped off to sleep in mid-sentence. I sighed and gripped the steering wheel trying to keep the truck on the road. It would be a long drive with no one to talk to but I didn't have the heart to wake him.

A while later we came to the river town with the hamburger joint that served the huge burgers. His eyes popped open like he had radar. "You are planning to stop," he said. "You know how hungry catching all those fish made me, don't you? And besides, we have to stop anyway...you owe me an ice-cream."

There's only one thing that Thunderfoot likes better than walleye fishing, and that's eating on the road to and from walleye fishing.

Thanks, Thunderfoot.

A Bit Early for a Dip

"I just rode my bike down to the river and the water temperature is over fifty degrees," Thunderfoot said as he slid to a stop in my driveway. "Do you think the smallmouths will be biting?"

"How far over fifty?" I asked.

"It was only fifty-two but the sun's out and they should be up in shallow water where it's warmer."

I was impressed. After the time we'd spent fishing together he was actually learning a lot about fishing. It seemed that fifty degrees was the magic temperature in the Wisconsin River. In the fall as soon as the water temperature dropped below fifty, the smallmouths seemed to disappear. Then in the spring the reverse happened. As soon as the water temperatures get in the fifty degree range, the smallmouths begin to bite again, just like clockwork. And, Thunderfoot and I loved fishing for smallmouths.

"Don't you think we should go and try for some?" he asked.

"Sure, I think it would be our duty to go," I said. "Unfortunately I have to finish this raking."

He looked like a cat caught in a live-trap. He shook his head and walked to the shed and grabbed a rake. "They *better* be biting," he said.

A couple of hours later we slid the boat into the river and motored upstream. We stopped at some rocky shorelines that were usually good smallmouth haunts. Thunderfoot was sitting in the front seat grinning. "There's nothing better than catching that first smallmouth of the season," he said. He tied a small spinner on his line and cast toward the rocks. I tied a small bait on my line and tossed it toward the shore. I had only turned the reel handle twice when I had a jarring strike. A nice smallie leaped into the air and then made a swift run up against the current. The fish came up again and jumped and then I led it to

114

the boat, lipped it and held it up for Thunderfoot to see. He glared at me.

"Jeez, you didn't hardly give me time to fish."

I grinned and he cast right to the same place my fish had come from and caught the twin brother of my fish. "All righty then," he said.

We moved a little way downriver and began casting again. Thunderfoot's spinner had no more than hit the water when he reared back and set the hook. "I think I've died and gone to heaven," he said.

It was an amazing start to an amazing day of fishing. We cast the entire rocky shore and then went back upriver and did it again. We caught a total of eleven bass and one walleye on that shoreline and then went to look for a similar spot. As we motored up the river Thunderfoot sat in his seat with a smile on his face as we looked for another hot-spot. There wasn't much more you could have given him just then that would have made him happier than he was right now.

"Let's try over there," he said pointing to some rocks sticking up along the shore. I pulled the boat to a stop above the rocks and cast back to them, hooking a fish right away. "That's pretty greedy of you," he said.

"That's the advantage of being the boat driver," I said grinning.

Like the previous spot, this one was full of fish. About halfway through our first drift Thunderfoot hauled back and set the hook into a much bigger fish than we had been catching. This fish stripped off line and took off for the middle of the river. "This is a world record smallmouth," he said as he struggled with the fish. He did a really good job of fighting the fish and soon a huge northern was lying on the surface beside the boat. Thunderfoot lifted it up by the gill plate and held it up for me to see. "I'm a multi-species angler," he said proudly. Then he removed the lure from the fish and slid it back into the river. "This is going to be one of those days to remember," he said.

We fished the new shoreline for about an hour and then decided to move again. "Why don't you let me drive?" he said. "You can relax and enjoy the scenery."

I knew he wasn't concerned about me enjoying the scenery as much as he wanted to control the boat on the next spot, but I agreed and let him drive. Soon we saw another likely looking spot and in addition to the rocks, this spot had tree tops that had fallen into the water. This was going to be a good spot for sure.

Thunderfoot pulled in on the spot and managed to position the boat so he was nearer the shore and I was out in the middle of the river.

"How do you expect me to cast?" I asked. "You've got the boat sitting so I don't have anywhere to fish but the middle of the river."

He looked at me innocently. "Oh, can't you cast? I'm real sorry." Then he cast to a nearby log and hooked a bass. He turned around with an evil grin as he reeled in the fish.

I wasn't going to sit and watch him catch all the fish so I stood up and climbed up onto the deck on the front of the boat so I could cast over him. "You'd better be careful...you might fall in," he said.

It wasn't ten seconds later, that the boat hit an underwater log. We were traveling along with the current at a pretty good rate, so when we hit the log I did a back flip off the front of the boat in less time than it took to type this sentence. I landed on m back and as I hit, my rod and reel came loose from my grip and was gone. The water felt like ice. I was under water and not sure which way was up because it all happened to fast. I wasn't afraid so I just let myself drop down until I hit bottom. I had spent my entire youth in the river and knew that all I had to do was go with the current and I'd be ok. Once I hit bottom, I knew which way was up. I pushed off and swam to the surface.

When I popped up at the surface Thunderfoot was in a panic. "Holy cow...are you ok?"

"Yeah, I'm alright, I lost my rod and reel though. I'll swim down to that sandbar, you come and pick me up," I said.

He started the motor and I waded into the shallow water at the sandbar. He stopped and I climbed into the boat. "Holy cow, I thought you were caught under a snag or something and had drowned," he said. "You were under the water for hours."

"I don't think it was hours. I didn't know which way was up, so I had to wait till I got to the bottom. Let's go back and see if we can find my rod and reel."

We motored up the shoreline and lo and behold, my lure was hanging from a branch in a treetop. Thunderfoot motored up so I cold grab the lure and then I began pulling up the line and soon my rod and reel came up from the bottom of the river. "It's good you can't cast very well," he said laughing. "If you'd hit your target your rod would still be on the bottom."

By now I was getting pretty chilly. It was late in the afternoon and the sun was low on the horizon. "I hate to say this but I'm freezing and we've got along way to go to get home. I think we should call it quits for today," I said.

He looked a little disappointed the then smiled. "I told you we'd remember this day, and now that you did that nice back flip I'm sure of it."

My teeth were chattering by the time we got the boat loaded. When we got home I jumped in the shower and warmed up. Thunderfoot came into the house as I finished dressing. He had put away the gear and had a grin on his face.

"So, when are you leaving for training camp?"

"What do you mean?" I asked smiling.

"I mean to try out for the Olympic diving team. I'd give you at least a nine point five on that back flip."

Wasn't that nice of him?

Thanks, Thunderfoot.

Who's Smarter Now?

I was driving as fast as you dare to drive in the darkness in deer country toward our turkey hunting woods. Thunderfoot was stuffing shells and other gear into our fanny packs.

"We should have gotten up about half an hour earlier," I said. "I don't know if we can make it to the top of the hill before the birds wake up." Thunderfoot gave me a worried look.

We had been out the two previous mornings and had heard turkeys gobbling from their roost trees so we knew where to go. But we had miscalculated on our time this morning and we were probably going to be late. We pulled into the driveway of the abandoned farm where we hunted and quietly got out of the pickup. We were careful not to slam the doors and wake up the whole neighborhood. Thunderfoot got his gun out of the case and slid a big three-and-a-half inch shell into the chamber of the ten-gauge. He carefully closed the breech and made sure the hammer was down in the safe position. Then we picked up the decoys and the rest of the gear and started across the field toward the hill.

It was still pretty dark but the sky was beginning to turn into a dark blue in the east as we climbed the hill. We had to be very quiet because we had to pass within about fifty yards of the roost trees to get to the top of the hill. We were hoping that the birds would go up the hill when they left their roosts later.

Thunderfoot knew where we were going and was leading the way. He kept looking up at the sky that was getting brighter and brighter by the minute. I was right behind him when he let a branch go that slapped me right across the left ear.

"Jeez!" I whispered. "Take it easy. You almost took my ear off." I was rubbing my smarting ear and saw his grin in the darkness.

"Sorry," he said. "It slipped."

By the time we got to the top of the hill it was fully light. We heard the noise as the turkeys flew down from their roosts. We crept up behind a little knoll and peeked over. The turkeys were standing right next to the brush pile we had planned on sitting behind. "Oh great," I whispered. "Lie down and get the gun ready. I'll try to call them." I was panting from the climb and excited at being so close to the birds.

Thunderfoot lay down next to a big oak and I pulled my favorite diaphragm call out of my call box. I gave a seductive yelp. The turkeys stopped walking and craned their necks listening. I waited a few minutes and they began moving away. I called again and they completely ignored me.

We lay there for a quite a while and finally I rolled over and looked at Thunderfoot. "Well we blew that one. Tomorrow we'll be here at least half an hour earlier."

He nodded in agreement. We sat and called and listened for three hours but there were no interested turkeys in our woods. "We might as well go home," I said. "We'll leave the decoys and camouflage netting here so we don't have to carry it all back up here tomorrow. I put the decoys in the brush pile and covered them with the camo netting and we left for the day.

The next morning we were on top of the hill almost an hour earlier than the previous day. We had the decoys out and our blind built long before any turkey would even think of gobbling and beginning his day.

"Today we score," Thunderfoot said. "They don't have a clue that we're here."

I felt pretty smug also. We both leaned back against a log and waited for light to come. The sky brightened and suddenly a turkey gobbled on the next hill over from the one we were on. Then another gobbled from the same area. I expected "our" turkeys to answer them from just below us, but there wasn't a peep from our hill.

Thunderfoot looked at me. "You don't suppose those are our birds do you?"

I shrugged my shoulders and motioned to just wait for a

while. After another ten minutes of listening to turkeys gobble all around us, I decided to try a call on my diaphragm. I called. No response. I called again. No response.

The birds on the other hill were carrying on like crazy. We sat there looking kind of glum. "They moved to the other hill," Thunderfoot said dejectedly.

I nodded. "We might was well sit here for now," I said. "If we try to get over there they'll see us anyway."

The next morning we hauled all the gear up the side of the hill next to the one we had been on the day before. This hill was nearly vertical. We were following a path that had been made many years earlier when the gas company buried its pipeline. There wasn't much brush and there were a lot of loose rocks to work around as we climbed. We were trying not to launch any rocks down the hill which would scare the turkeys we were stalking.

I was sweating and huffing and puffing and thought I'd keel over at any minute. Finally we got to the top and I sat down to get my breath.

"Those birds better be there today after all of this," I panted.

We found a spot to hide and got ready for daylight. After about ten minutes we heard a turkey calling from the next hill down the line. "I can't believe it," I said.

Our birds had moved again. For some reason they had roosted on another hill rather than on the one they had used the day before. We were not having very good luck and were running out of time and hills. There was only one more hill in that valley that was still on the land we were hunting. If they moved off onto other land we'd be out of luck.

The next morning we decided to try the next hill though it was foreign to us. We'd never been this far south on the farm, so we were kind of hunting blind. This new hill turned out to be the steepest of the bunch. Even Thunderfoot was panting when we got to the top. We didn't know exactly where to go so we naturally picked the wrong spot. We settled down in a little corner of a field and placed our decoys at about twenty yards. I began calling and got little response.

"I guess we'll just stay put and try to call one over from one of the other hills," I said. Thunderfoot was less than enthusiastic, but we didn't have much choice.

I called every ten minutes or so and heard a gobble after about half an hour. I kept calling and suddenly Thunderfoot whispered. "There he is!"

I looked and saw a tom standing on top of the hill about a hundred yards away. He was looking at our decoys, but he didn't seem convinced that they were real. Try as I might I couldn't get him to come any closer. I tried every trick I knew but he finally just walked slowly back into the woods.

Thunderfoot breathed a long sigh. "Now what?"

"Let's leave the gear here. Tomorrow instead of setting up here we'll set up right on top of the hill where he was today. Then we'll see who's smarter."

Thunderfoot looked like he was going to say something but decided not to. We took off for home.

The next morning was our last chance. We got to the top of the hill right on schedule. I must have been getting into shape because the hill seemed less difficult to climb each day. If the season was 6 months long, I'd be an Olympian. We picked up our gear and placed the decoys in the field where the tom had been the previous day. I turned to see where Thunderfoot was sitting and couldn't see him. I looked and looked and then I saw him wave from the brush pile. I crawled into the pile and sat down just behind him.

Thunderfoot was resting the ten-gauge on a log that was in just the right place in our little blind. The brush pile had been pushed there by a bulldozer some years back and was a combination of branches and logs all piled up.

"This is a good spot," he whispered. "Just let him show his face and he's mine."

When it got light we heard gobbling all around us, but none

that was really close. I began to call every few minutes without much response from any of the toms. This went on for about an hour.

"Where the heck did they all go?" Thunderfoot asked.

I was going to lean forward to answer him when something caught my eye from the right. I turned my head just a fraction of an inch and saw a tom standing to the right of us, about fifty yards away.

"Don't move," I whispered. "There's a tom on the right about fifty yards out."

The bird stood there for a while and then took a couple of steps toward the decoys. He stayed on the edge of the field just out of range. I saw Thunderfoot turn his head a bit so he cold se the bird. The tom would take a few steps and then stop and eat some alfalfa or pick at something on the ground. Then it would move a little closer to the decoys, always just out of range.

Thunderfoot moved the gun around very slowly so it was pointed at the bird. I saw the barrel begin to waver as he tried to hold the big gun up and keep it on the turkey.

Finally the tom looked right at us and then stood as tall as he could and then looked some more. He brought his neck back down and took a step backwards.

"Uh oh," I said. "He saw something he didn't like."

"What should I do?" Thunderfoot whispered.

"I don't know. I don't think he's gong to come any closer. I'm guessing he's about forty-five yards out. That gun can reach him. If he looks like he's going to run, blast him."

The turkey stood rock still for several minutes then turned and took a step to the right. Thunderfoot touched off the big gun just as he raised his other leg to take a step. The turkey's next step was a leap straight up into the air. He took off for the woods with Thunderfoot in hot pursuit. He jumped up and ran after the turkey the instant after he fired the gun. I was trying to get up from my nest in the brush pile. My legs had fallen asleep from sitting so long.

Soon Thunderfoot came back over the top of the hill shaking his head. "Not a feather," he said.

I decided to pace off the distance. Thunderfoot followed counting steps. When we got to where the turkey had been standing we found it had been almost sixty yards. "No wonder," I said. "He was a lot farther out that we thought."

"It was pretty exciting when he came in silent like that," he said. "At least I got to shoot the gun."

He handed me a juice box that he had taken from his pack. "Here can you open this?" His hands were shaking.

I grinned. "No bird but we had a little excitement huh?"

"Yeah, and we sure found out who's smarter didn't we?"

I never claimed to be a genius.

Thanks, Thunderfoot.

The Rabbit

I was puttering around in the yard on one of the first really warm days of spring when Thunderfoot came up my driveway on his new riding lawnmower.

"I thought maybe I'd mow your grass for you," he said looking over the yard.

I looked around at the new grass which was barely two inches tall. "Don't you think it's a little short yet?

"Nope, I think I better cut it. It's kind of uneven, I'll just shape it up for you. This way if we want to go fishing later in the week, we won't have to worry about the grass getting too long," he said as he lowered the cutting head and started across the yard.

Now if the truth be known, Thunderfoot wasn't all that worried about the quality of my lawn, or future fishing trips. His mom had just bought the new rider after years of him pestering her for one, and he was trying to keep the machine running day and night. He had mowed their grass so many times that his mom forbade him to do it again. He loved driving the new toy and my lawn was a good excuse to get it moving again. He was like most teenage boys. He was at that age where he thought he just had to have something to drive, and if it was a lawnmower, so be it.

He was merrily riding back and forth across my lawn, so I went back to my puttering. Occasionally he'd yell at me to watch and he's stop, rev up the engine and try to pop-a-wheelie. I just shook my head, so obvious was his derangement.

He finished an hour later and we went into the house for some lunch. It started to rain while we were eating so he hurried up so he could get his "wheels" home and into the garage so it wouldn't get wet.

I cleaned up from lunch and settled down with a book. It was a perfect afternoon to do nothing and I was doing just that. The windows were open and the smell of a spring rain drifted into the living room making it very peaceful and relaxing. It must have been very relaxing because in no time I was sleeping quite soundly with my book in my lap.

Suddenly I woke with a start as someone pounded on my front door. I got up and walked to the door and it was Thunderfoot, who was standing on the front porch. I opened the door and looked at him. "Why didn't you just come in?" I asked.

He had a terrified look on his face. "You better come out here, I'm kind of muddy."

I looked down at his feet and his shoes and pant legs were covered with mud. He was soaking wet the rest of the way up and he was sweating and panting like he had just run a marathon.

"I buried the Rabbit," he panted.

"You what? What rabbit?"

"Mom's Rabbit. I buried it down by the lake."

I was still trying to figure out what he was talking about.

"Mom's gone for the day, so I kind of borrowed her Rabbit and took it for a spin. You know where the road is kind of low and there's usually a big mud puddle there? Well, I went ramming into that puddle and half way through the Rabbit died."

Now I knew what he was talking about. His mom had an old VW Rabbit which she had used before she bought her new car. The Rabbit was just sitting in the driveway not being used and Thunderfoot had taken it for a joyride.

"What the heck were you doing driving the Rabbit? Are you crazy?"

He hung his head.

"How did you get back here from the lake?"

"I ran."

"You ran? That's three miles."

He looked at me pleadingly. "Please, don't start. I know I shouldn't have taken it but I did, so that part is done. I need you to help me get it out of the mud puddle and back home so mom doesn't find out. She'll never let me get my driver's license until I'm like eighty years old if she does."

I was hesitant to become part of this little conspiracy but I could see the terror in his eyes. I was kind of touched that he came to me for help too, so I said I'd help him. "Under one condition," I said.

"Anything."

"Promise me you'll never take that car again or any car, until you're old enough to get your license and drive."

"I won't even walk close to it," he said.

I went to the phone and called a friend of mine who had a long chain and he agreed to meet me down by the lake. Thunderfoot and I got into the pickup and drove down through the river bottoms road to the lake. We came to the low spot in the road and sure enough, there was a huge mud puddle. The spring thaw had filled the low spot that was about fifty yards long with water and mud. Sitting almost exactly in the middle of the puddle was the drowned Rabbit. It was quite a sight. The poor Rabbit was covered with mud from top to bottom. If the puddle had been an inch or two deeper the car would have had mud running in through the doors also.

"Boy, you did a good job of it," I said.

Thunderfoot shook his head mournfully.

I stopped near the puddle and put on my hip boots as did my friend who had just arrived. Then I drove slowly toward the Rabbit with my 4-wheel drive engaged. My friend waded along with the chain and attached it to the bumper of the Rabbit. I tightened up the chain and began towing the Rabbit back to dry ground.

Once it was out of the puddle, my friend got in and started the Rabbit. Then he drove it back to Thunderfoot's house and parked it exactly where Thunderfoot directed him. We went back to get his truck while Thunderfoot set out to clean up the Rabbit so his mom wouldn't notice.

I dropped my friend off as his truck, thanked him for his help and went home.

A while later I saw Thunderfoot's mom go past on her way

home. I felt a little guilty for helping him deceive her but hoped it would be a good lesson for him.

A while later Thunderfoot came walking glumly into m living room. "Busted!" he said.

"Busted? I thought you cleaned it all up."

He sat down and shook his head. "I did...well I thought I did. I had my brother help and he was doing the top parts while I did the bottom. He missed a big stripe right down the middle of the roof. It looked like a brown racing stripe. Mom saw it as soon as she pulled into the driveway."

I couldn't help but laugh. "Well, we tried," I said. "Was she mad?"

"Oh she was plenty mad. But when she found out that you had helped me she really got mad."

Oh boy.

Thanks, Thunderfoot.

Great America

"Mom's taking me and my brother to Great America for my birthday. Do you want to come along?" Thunderfoot asked as he walked into the house.

"Great America...isn't that some kind of amusement park?"

"Yeah, it's really a cool place. They have all kind of neat rides and roller coasters and stuff."

I wasn't too sure about roller coasters. I had made it to this point in my life without feeling a necessity to ride a roller coaster and wasn't sure I wanted to change that. "Why do you want me to go?"

"Well, my brother is too short to get on some of the rides, so I want someone to go so I have someone to ride with. Mom won't go on them, so I was hoping you'd go along."

"Why won't your mom ride on them?

He hesitated. "Well, she doesn't want Caleb to have to wait by himself while we ride. She's scared somebody might steal him or something."

Well I guess that made sense.

"Please say you'll go. We'll have a lot of fun, I promise."

It was his birthday and I did enjoy spending time with him and his family so I agreed to go along. We left bright and early the following Saturday. "We want to get there early so we get our money's worth," he said.

As soon as we left town Thunderfoot and Caleb were fast asleep in the back seat. His mom and I talked about the usual stuff on the road and sometime later the subject of roller coasters came up. She seemed pretty surprised that I had agreed to ride them with Thunderfoot.

"You've never seen them have you?" she asked.

"I've seen the ads on TV, but no, I've never seen an actual roller coaster," I admitted.

She just grinned.

A while later you could see the tops of the roller coaster tracks from the highway several miles away from the park. My stomach began to quiver as I watched little colorful cars full of screaming people hurtle up and down the tracks. When we got to the park Thunderfoot and Caleb were off and running for the entrance as soon as we had parked the car.

We all got our tickets and walked into the park which was teeming with people of all ages, sizes and colors, going one way or the other in a seemingly huge hurry. There was a giant merry-go-round just inside the entrance that was playing loud circus music and screams filled the air from the direction of the first roller coaster.

"Let's try the Shock Wave first....it's right over that way," Thunderfoot said motioning for me to follow him. His mom smiled and said she and Caleb were going on some of the smaller rides and they'd catch up with us later.

As we approached the line of people waiting to get on the Shock Wave, my stomach began to feel like it had a couple of bowling balls rolling around in it. The line followed back and forth in some stanchion-like walkways. Once you got in line and more people filled in behind you, it was pretty hard to change your mind and leave without making a lot of people move out of the way.

Thunderfoot was merrily chattering with a couple of kids ahead of us in line. I began looking around and saw that not only were there kids, but also there were lots of adults and even a grandma or two. Hmm, maybe this wouldn't be so bad after all.

We went through the first enclosure and up some steps. Suddenly a roar came from overhead as one of the little cars hurtled past filled with screaming people. The car shot past us, spun in a loop and then turned upside-down in a series of spirals before continuing on down the track. I stood there with my mouth hanging open watching the car disappear into the distance when I felt someone tugging on my sleeve. It was Thunderfoot.

129

"You're holding up the line," he said gesturing at the people behind me that looked impatiently at me. I looked ahead and there was a big gap in the line caused by me standing there like a dimwit. I wasn't sure I wanted to move up but I sure didn't want to wade back through a few hundred people in the stanchions to get out of there either, so I followed Thunderfoot.

We kept moving forward until we got to the "loading station" where half a dozen college kids clad in bright blue jumpsuits merrily loaded passengers into the waiting "trains". They made sure each passenger was locked in and then all gave a cheery "thumbs-up" and off we went.

Thunderfoot's eyes were sparkling as we got close to the front of the line. "Don't worry, this is really fun," he said. I could only nod. My mouth was as dry as dust and I didn't think I could speak.

Finally we were first in line and our train came in. The survivors from the previous ride climbed out of their seats and it was our turn. I sat in the seat next to Thunderfoot and we pulled down the restraining bar that was suppose to keep us from being hurled out into the parking lot as the train rocketed down the tracks. A cheery girl checked our bar and gave us a hearty thumbs-up and off we went.

The train started with a jerk and then we moved from the station and turned a corner right away. After the corner we began climbing the first hill. It was very steep and we clattered along up and up and up toward the top of the track. I peeked over the side and could see the parking lot a long, long way down.

"This is real cool," Thunderfoot exclaimed. I just nodded.

We climbed and climbed and finally reached the top. For a couple of seconds we just hung there. Then we started down the other side, our speed increasing each second. Half way down the hill we tipped on our side and increased speed even more. We were headed toward the earth on our side when I gripped the restraining bar and began screaming like a ten-year-old girl. My stomach seemed to rise up and I expected it to pop out of my mouth at any second. We got to the bottom of the first hill, and immediately headed into a series of loops that took us upside down three or four times, and then into a series of corkscrew spins. I think there were more loops after that but my memory is kind of fuzzy from there on. I think I was holding my breath and had a small brain meltdown due to lack of oxygen. My body was preparing for shut-down and eternity.

Then, just as suddenly as the whole thing had started, the car jerked to a stop and we were back at the station. The smiling college girl came over to release our restraint bar but I was gripping it so tightly she couldn't budge it. My fingers were frozen to the bar.

"You gotta let go," Thunderfoot said. I nodded and pried my fingers loose. I couldn't talk because my throat was cramped up from the way I had tightened it during the ride in an effort to keep my stomach from flying out into space.

I finally staggered to my feet and followed Thunderfoot down the exit ramp. He was babbling excitedly about the next rids and how it was even better than the Shock Wave. When we got to the exit there were lines of people looking at TV monitors that showed people on the ride as they went over the first hill in stop-motion.

"Come and see this," Thunderfoot said laughing.

"What's this?" I asked.

"They've got a camera on the first drop. It takes your picture as you go by."

Soon we saw our car come into view and then slowly each pair of riders went past. Thunderfoot was laughing with his hands in the air and I was looking like I was about to expire, my hands gripped on the bar, my hair flying, and a look of terror on my face. My mouth was wide open making me look quite mad.

"We can buy that for only five dollars," Thunderfoot said.

"I think I'll pass. I'd never hear the end of it if you have proof of how bad I looked."

I walked over to a bench and sat down, still a little wobbly.

"What did you think of it?" Thunderfoot asked.

"Well, it was pretty bad, but I guess it was kind of fun too. I guess that if those little kids and grannies can do it, I can too."

"Cool, the next one's even better."

"Even better? What does that mean...even better?"

"Well there're seven coasters in the park. We started at the least scary one. So they get better all day long."

Oh boy, I could hardly wait.

Thanks, Thunderfoot.

The Fishing Was Hot

It was one of those hot summer days where you could work up a sweat just sitting still. I had worked all day in the heat and humidity and was now relaxing after a shower. My recliner was tipped back and I was soaking up the air-conditioning, when Thunderfoot came through the front door. He was carrying his fishing pole and his hair was wet and matted against his head with sweat.

"Whew...it's hot out there," he said. "You know this is one of those days when the northerns will just about jump into the boat don't you?"

I shook my head. "It's way too hot to go fishing."

He looked at me in disbelief. "I didn't mean go now...I meant a little while later when the sun starts to go down. Then it'll be a lot cooler."

"It's going to have to cool down a whole lot to get me outside again today," I said as I flipped on the TV to watch the evening news.

Thunderfoot went to the refrigerator and rummaged around until he found something he liked. Then he sat down on the couch and tried to look interested in the television. The weather-lady came on and told us of an impending storm front that would be passing through at any time and that it would cool off as the front passed. Thunderfoot heard that and looked at me nodding his head up and down.

I sighed. I knew he would bug me until I went fishing so I told him to get the gear ready and I'd be out in a minute. He took off like a shot to the garage to get the fishing gear ready. I turned off the TV and grudgingly got up from my recliner. When I walked outside it was like walking into a wet blanket of hot, moist air.

We loaded the johnboat into the back of the pickup and started off for our favorite river bottom slough. Ten minutes later we were sliding the boat down a sandy bank and into the water.

Sweat ran into my eyes as I paddled toward the main part of the lake. Thunderfoot was in the front casting to logs and lily pads along the way trying to be the first to catch a fish. On about his fourth cast he let out a whoop and hooked into a nice northern. The battle was on and after a good fight the fish was soon lying quietly at the side of the boat. Thunderfoot led the fish back to where I could reach it and I took it off the hook and released it.

"I told you," he said grinning.

As much as I hated to admit it I knew he was right. For some unknown reason the fish seemed to bite like crazy on hot humid days like this one. Something about the heat and humidity turned them on and if you could stand the fishing conditions, you would usually have a great day of fishing. This was definitely going to be one of those days.

We paddled into the main part of the lake and a slight breeze came up. We paddled to the end where the breeze was coming from and let it take us back down the lake slowly. As we drifted along we started catching fish after fish. One of us was fighting a fish almost all the time. We often both had one on at once. It was really lots of fun, so when we got to the end of the lake we paddled back upwind and did it again.

This went on for about an hour and a half at which time we began to hear thunder off in the west. I looked and there were some pretty big ugly black storm clouds coming our way. They were still quite a way off so we kind of ignored them.

When we got to the downwind end of the lake again we started back to the other end. "Those storm clouds are getting pretty close," I said. "Maybe we should start back to the shore."

"We've got time for another drift," Thunderfoot said. "It won't take long to get to shore."

We started another drift but the thunder was getting louder and louder. The clouds were getting blacker and uglier by the minute. Suddenly a huge bolt of lightning cracked and it was very close. It was followed by a deafening clap of thunder.

"That's it," I said, "Roll up your line, we're out of here."

Thunderfoot didn't argue and looked uneasily at the sky as he reeled in his line. About half way back, a fish struck his lure. He looked over his shoulder at me and shrugged. "I didn't do that on purpose," he said.

I picked up my paddle and began moving us toward the shore. The wind picked up and now it was blowing hard right in our faces. We had to go into the wind for quite a long way before we could turn and go into the bank. Lightning began snapping all around us and the thunder was booming. "Get that fish off your line and lay your pole down in the boat," I yelled. "Holding that rod up in the air like that is just like holding a lightning rod."

For once, Thunderfoot didn't argue with me. He horsed the fish in and laid his rod in the boat after quickly releasing the fish. He was looking kind of worried as he picked up his paddle and helped me move us toward the bank. We reached the shore just as it started raining. I say raining because I don't know a word for what it was doing. It was actually like being under a waterfall. The rain was coming down so hard that there weren't individual drops, just large sheets of it hammering us. And, of course, for good measure, the wind picked up to gale force at the same time.

We each grabbed an end of the boat and carried it up the embankment through the maelstrom. We slid the boat into the back of the truck and ran for the cab just as the hail began to beat down on us.

We were panting while we waited for the windows to clear up from the fog and Thunderfoot said, "Maybe one less drift would have been more prudent."

I laughed. "No kidding, that's the understatement of the year."

I could finally see well enough to drive so I started down the dirt road through the woods that led back to the highway. Thunderfoot was wiping the fog off the back window when he suddenly yelled out. "Holy smokes! A big tree just fell across the road right behind the truck!"

I looked out at the mirror and sure enough a large old oak tree was lying in the road where we had been just seconds earlier. "Wow, that was close," I said. "A minute or two earlier and we'd have been trapped in here or crushed."

"If it had trapped us, we could have just stayed all night and fished for our supper," Thunderfoot said grinning. He loved the thought of any adventure like that.

We slowly made our way home and when we got to the driveway we made a run for the house. "We'll put the boat away after the storm passes," I said as I ran inside. Thunderfoot was right behind me. Of course there wasn't any reason to hurry because we were soaked to the skin already anyway.

"Jeez, it's like a freezer in here," he said wrapping his arms around his wet chest.

I went to the bathroom and grabbed a couple of towels and some dry clothes from my closet and "his" room. We dried off and changed into dry clothes and felt much better.

"That was pretty cool," he said. "Boy, we sure got the fish didn't we? And we almost got blown away by the storm. And we got really wet too. And now I don't even have to take a shower."

That boy could find good in almost any situation.

Thanks, Thunderfoot.

Goodbye to Sophie

Anyone who has ever loved a dog be it a hunting companion or a lap dog, knows how hard it is to watch them get old and sick. Dogs are much more than pets. They are much more than a helper that fetches game for you. They are a friend, and are loved very much. When the time comes at the end of their life, when you have to make the decision to have them put to sleep, it just about tears your heart out. That was the dilemma I was facing with my dear old Sophie. She had cancer and was failing badly. Her time was near and I was dreading it more than anything.

Thunderfoot also knew that his old friend was sick. Try as he might he couldn't coax her for more than one fetch of the tennis ball anymore. He came over and we talked about what needed to be done and I told him I had called my vet and she was coming in the morning. Thunderfoot sat quietly for a while and then said he was going home. He stopped and petted Sophie a few minutes and then hurried out with his eyes brimming with tears.

The next morning he came over with a small plastic bag in his hand. He sat down by Sophie and gave her a chew-bone. Her tail thumped on the floor as he hugged her and petted her for the last time. His eyes were full of tears and he came and hugged me and then left for school. My heart was nearly breaking as I watched him saying goodbye to his old pal.

Later that morning Dr. Pat arrived and my dear sweet Sophie's suffering was over very gently and quickly. My heart was aching as I dug a grave in the back yard near Sophie's mom and grandma. I wrapped her in a blanket and put the chew bone Thunderfoot had given her inside with her. When I was done, I pretty much just let the rest of the day go by without doing much of anything.

After school Thunderfoot came walking across the back yard from his house. I saw him glance over in the yard at the fresh earth of Sophie's grave. He sat down next to me on the couch and sighed. He turned to look at me and his eyes were brimming full of tears.

"It was really peaceful," I said. "Dr. Pat just put the shot in and Sophie was looking at me and then she just closed her eyes and she was gone."

He smiled and put his arms around me and we hugged for a long time. "Well, now what?" he asked.

"I guess we better start looking for a dog," I said.

"Are you sure?"

"It's going to be way to quiet and you know how used to dog hair I've become."

He smiled, and headed home.

The next morning I heard the refrigerator door open just after dawn. I got out of bed to see what was going on and there was Thunderfoot sitting at the table eating cereal with the newspaper opened to the Want Ads. "The paperboy just left the newspaper a while ago and I saw an ad for golden retriever pups," he said as he shoveled cereal into his face. He had circled the ad and I read it while I got the waffle maker out and began whipping up some batter.

It was Saturday and he didn't have school so we decided to go look at the puppies after breakfast. He was really excited about it but then he stopped and looked seriously at me. "This isn't too soon is it? I mean, I don't want you to think I'm forgetting Sophie already. I'll never forget her."

I put my arm around his shoulder and hugged him. "We won't ever forget Sophie. This puppy, if we get one, will be another new adventure for us to share. We had a great time with Sophie and we made memories we'll always keep in our hearts. She'll always be with us." He smiled and hugged me back.

After breakfast we loaded up in the pickup and drove to the address where the puppies were located. I told him we were just going to look and not to get too excited about bringing a puppy home with us. We might want to think about it a while before we made a decision.

When we pulled into the driveway of the address from the paper we saw a kennel in the back yard and a pile of sleeping puppies. A huge grin spread over Thunderfoot's face as we approached the pen. The sleeping puppies began waking up and climbing over each other all vying for the attention of these strangers. I knocked on the door and a teenaged boy came out of the house and offered to let the puppies out so we could look at them. When he unlocked the door of the kennel it was like a rain barrel had tipped over and a flood of puppies rolled out of the pen. There were nine of them and they were all over us in an instant. They were tugging at shoe laces and Thunderfoot had knelt down so he had three puppies pulling on his shirttail. He was already picking them up checking for girls but as soon as he put one down, it mixed with the others and it was impossible to figure out who was who. The boy from the house started putting male puppies back in the pen much to their dismay. They whined and barked at being left out of the fun. One of the females had a little blue collar and was spoken for already. We were left with four females to choose from. Thunderfoot played with the "girls" and soon one stood out from the others. She was determined to get Thunderfoot's shoe laces untied and as quickly as he took her away from them she went right back for more. I could tell he was falling in love.

"That's the one my little sister likes best too," the boy said.

Thunderfoot picked up the little blond fur ball and hugged her. "This one's a sweetie," he said kissing the puppy on the nose.

I sighed. I should have known that if we saw puppies we'd be going home with one. It's not that I didn't want one but I felt just a little guilty with Sophie so recently gone. On the other hand I knew there was no way we were leaving that pup behind, so I told the teenager we'd take her and he went to get the papers. Thunderfoot took the pup to the pen so she could say goodbye to her family and we headed out down the road toward home.

The puppy wasn't real happy about her first ride in a truck.

She was obviously frightened so Thunderfoot picked her up and held her in his arms like a baby. She settled down and went right to sleep. "She's just so beautiful," he said beaming. "And she looks really smart too." I just smiled.

After we got home Thunderfoot and the puppy took off for the back yard to play. I watched them romping and playing fetch and knew we had done the right thing

"What are we going to call her?" I said.

A serious look came over his face. "Gosh, I don't know. It has to be something just right."

He looked at the puppy. She was jumping up and down waiting for him to start playing again. "I just love her, that's for sure."

"What about Lucy?" I said.

"Lucy?"

"Yeah, like you said...you love her. Kind of like 'I Love Lucy'."

He broke into a huge grin. "Lucy...I love Lucy. Cool."

Soon the puppy was tired out and she laid down under the picnic table for a nap. We sat down at the table and watched her sleep.

After a while Thunderfoot got up and walked over to Sophie's grave and squatted down. He sat there for a while and I could see he was talking to Sophie. Then he patted the ground gently and walked back. "I told Soph about the puppy and I told her we really miss her. I told her we'll never forget her.'

He looked down at the puppy sleeping and grinned. "She looks like a little angel."

Finally he got up and started for home. He stopped and turned back to me. "You know, when you get to heaven I bet you'll find a lot of dogs there. That would be about the best thing I could think of...to be able to spend all eternity with your dogs. That's what heaven is...a whole lot of dogs."

I hope he's right.

Thanks, Thunderfoot.

Goodbye, Sophie.

Stumped

The longest duck season in many years had given Thunderfoot and me a chance to do some late season duck hunting on the Mississippi River. Our local duck ponds had long ago frozen over but the big river was still open and there were lots of migrating ducks using it. An old friend of mine owned a cottage on the riverbank just north of Lynxville and he and I had been talking the previous evening. The subject of the cottage came up and he informed me that there was no one using it next weekend, and I was welcome to it. It was perfect for a place to stay while we hunted late season ducks. I got the key to the cottage and called Thunderfoot.

"Are you crazy? What do you mean, do I want to go? How soon are we leaving?" I guess he thought it was a good idea. Ten minutes later he came running across the back yard with a duffel bag and his shotgun.

"Gus said we can use the boat at the cottage," I said, "and he has three dozen decoys in the shed. So all we need to take is our clothes and guns."

"And lunch," Thunderfoot corrected. "You know how hungry this late fall air makes me." Cold air, hot air, late fall air, any air made him hungry.

We got to the cottage as dusk and began getting the gear ready. "Check out the boat and make sure the plug is in it," I said. I went to the shed and found the decoys, oars, and life jackets and piled everything on the porch of the cottage. Thunderfoot was rummaging around in the boat, but soon he came over and helped me transfer the decoys from the porch to the boat.

We stood there on the bank of the big river and looked out across the black water. It was almost three miles to the Iowa side and as the light faded we watched several flocks of ducks settling onto the cold water.

"How are we gonna find the boat blind in the dark?" he asked.

I pointed across the water. "See those two yellow lights over there? Those are in Iowa and are right in line with the boat blind. We just steer for them and we should run right into it." Thunderfoot nodded that he understood.

That evening we made a sack of sandwiches and got the rest of our gear ready. We set the alarm for 4:15. I wanted to give us plenty of time to get across the river before it got light in the morning.

By about 4:30 the next morning we were setting out across the dark water toward the two little yellow lights. The small duck boat was loaded to the gills. We had three dozen decoys, our guns, eight boxes of shotgun shells in a waterproof box, lunch, hot chocolate, a gas heater, extra gloves and Lucy my golden retriever puppy. We were all packed into a small fiberglass boat pushed by a nine horsepower motor.

I watched the yellow lights and kept aiming for them. We slid through the water at a good rate and our beacons were getting closer and closer when we suddenly slammed to a halt.

Thunderfoot tipped over backwards off his seat. "Holy cow! What the heck happened?" he asked.

I grabbed the flashlight and pointed it over the side of the boat. We were sitting on top of a tree stump that was the size of a card table. It was about six inches under the water.

"Wow, I forgot, this is a stump field. I guess we found one of them," I said. "Take the oar and see if you can push us off."

Thunderfoot pushed and grunted but we were stuck fast. Finally I got up and carefully stepped over the side onto the stump and when the boat lightened, it slid back off the stump. I carefully got back to my seat and pulled the cord on the motor.

"Wow...that was thrilling. It's a good thing we're wearing hip boots or you would have gotten wet," he said.

We were getting close to the blind when Lucy suddenly climbed up onto Thunderfoot's lap.

"Lucy, get down," he said. "Hey, Lucy's all wet!"

"How did she get wet?" I asked.

Thunderfoot grabbed the flashlight and turned it on. He aimed it toward the bottom of the boat. It was three quarters full of water!

"Whoa! We're sinking, we're sinking!" he yelled.

I shut off the motor and grabbed an ice cream pail that was in the boat for bailing if needed, and we needed it right now. I began throwing water over the side as fast as I could.

"We must have punched a hole in the boat," I said. "We've got to get it bailed out and head for the nearest shore."

Thunderfoot sat there with the flashlight aimed at the floor of the boat. All of a sudden he let out a gasp and grabbed a piece of driftwood that was floating around in the water. He held it out to me. "Here, shove this back in the hole where the boat plug goes! This is the plug."

I grabbed the stick and pulled up my sleeve feeling around in the icy water for the hole for the plug. I finally found it and jammed the stick into the hole stopping the flood. Meanwhile Thunderfoot was bailing like mad. After a few minutes we were again floating safely.

"What pray tell, was that stick doing in the plug hole?" I asked.

"Well, I couldn't find the plug so I whittled that plug out of some driftwood on the shore while you were doing the other stuff. If you hadn't smacked into that stump at warp speed it would have been ok."

Now that the situation was at hand I had to laugh. It had been quite an exciting few minutes.

We continued on and a few yards later I could make out the form of the boat blind. My friend had built the blind so you could open one end and just drive the boat inside and hunt from the boat. It was on the edge of a big weed bed and a perfect place for hunting. We put out the decoys and positioned the boat in the blind just as the sky started to lighten. Soon after, the ducks began to fly.

Despite how badly the day had begun, it turned out to be an absolutely glorious morning. The sun came up and the ducks flew. Since it was so late in the season, we saw ducks that we'd never had a chance to hunt before. Many of these ducks were big-water ducks. They seldom used small ponds like we usually hunted, so we'd never had a chance at a shot at many kinds of them. Also these were the very late ducks that often came down from the north after the season had closed. We saw canvasbacks, redheads, golden eyes, blue bills, buffleheads, and hundreds of huge late mallards. Ducks flew up and down the river all day long. We had some of the greatest shooting we'd ever seen. By mid-afternoon we were one duck short of our limit. So, instead of shooting that last duck, we just sat in the boat and watched the ducks fly by and enjoyed the scene.

Finally I told Thunderfoot to pick one more duck and take it because it was getting late in the afternoon. "Let's get that last shot of the season and start back," I said. "I want to be past that stump field before it gets dark."

Thunderfoot shot the lead duck in a flock of blue bills and the day was over. We picked up the decoys and started back.

As we got to the area where we had hit the stump, he turned and looked at me. "Try not to slam into another stump...ok?"

I started to say something about we wouldn't have had any trouble if he'd found the real plug, but didn't bother. It had been a perfect day and I didn't want to spoil it with an argument. Besides, I usually lost those arguments anyway.

Thanks, Thunderfoot.

Let Them Get Close

"I really don't think it takes two of us to listen," Thunderfoot grumbled as he pulled his collar up over his head and slid down in the tall grass like a turtle withdrawing into his shell.

I had forced him to get up with me to "turkey listen", as he called it. Today was the morning before his turkey season would start. I wanted to hear the turkeys gobble when they woke up so we would know where to go the next morning. Turkeys usually roosted in nearly the same place each night, so knowing where they were this morning would give us a pretty good idea where they'd be tomorrow morning. Thunderfoot, on the other hand, thought this should be a one man operation and he should be home in his warm bed instead of out in the darkness.

I could just begin to make out the tops of the hills as the black sky turned to a dark blue when the first turkey gobbled. Thunderfoot sat up with a snap and looked at me, grinning from ear to ear.

"They're up by the corner of the field," he said nodding.

I nodded in agreement and soon we heard another gobble and then another. There seemed to be at least half a dozen turkeys in the area, so our chances seemed pretty good for the following morning.

Than night Thunderfoot stayed over at my house in "his room" which used to be my spare bedroom. We got up in plenty of time so we could be on top of the hill before light. We walked as cautiously and quietly as possible, so as not to disturb any roosting turkeys and climbed the hill.

When we reached the corner of the field I took our three decoys and placed them about twenty yards from the brush pile we were going to use for a blind. Thunderfoot cleared out the dead branches and was already sitting down when I got to the blind. I sat down in the only spot available and when it got light I found that I couldn't see the decoys. I mentioned that to

Thunderfoot and he whispered, "That's ok, I can see them and I'm the shooter anyway."

I took out my calls and we soon heard a gobbler not far off. I waited a short time and then made a soft, very sexy hen yelp. Thunderfoot looked over and winked his approval. A short time later the gobbler called again and I responded. This went on for about twenty minutes but then all was quiet.

We sat very still for quite a while and then Thunderfoot very slowly began raising the gun. I couldn't see a thing. He got the gun up to his shoulder and I heard him cock the hammer. I still couldn't see anything. He waited. I waited. Nothing happened. After what seemed like hours, he quietly lowered the gun and looked back at me. "Why didn't you tell me whether or not to shoot?"

"I didn't see him."

"Well, I didn't know if he was close enough."

"Where was he?"

"He was just to the left of the farthest decoy."

I leaned up far enough to see the decoy and knew the bird had been plenty close enough to shoot. "He was close enough," I said.

"Great, now you tell me," he said sarcastically.

"Next time, when they're by the decoys, you know they're close enough. But, if they're coming toward us, let them come. Each step they get closer to us is another step they have farther to go to get away from us." He nodded that he understood.

We waited a while longer and then decided to move up the ridge a little farther. There were turkeys calling all around us, so we thought a little move might help. As we moved the turkeys began gobbling all around us one after another. "Boy, we better sit down and get ready, we're surrounded," I said.

My heart was just about popping out of my chest by the time we got to the top of the ridge. We sat down in a little clearing. There were only two trees that were big enough to sit next to, so Thunderfoot took one and I the other which was a little way behind him. I was afraid to put out the decoys so we just sat down to wait.

"Remember, if he's coming closer, let him come," I whispered.

He nodded and laid the gun across his knees. It wasn't only a couple of minutes later when I saw a tom sneaking up to the side of us behind a brush pile. "There," I whispered. "Look behind the brush to your left."

The turkey was standing behind a downed tree and looking out over the top of the ridge. Nobody moved a muscle for many seconds and then the turkey suddenly ducked down and snuck off through the brush.

Thunderfoot slowly moved the gun back to the original place he had rested it and I slipped a turkey call into my mouth. I made a short yelp and almost swallowed the call when several toms answered immediately from just over the knoll. I didn't dare move and I could hardly breathe. Then I saw the head of a gobbler coming over the knoll right in front of us. He was only fifteen yards away. Right behind him was another gobbler and then another. There were three of them and they were all headed right at us. Although we were covered in camouflage from head to toe including our faces, I felt naked sitting against the tree with nothing between me and the turkeys but air.

The turkeys stretched their necks looking for the hen that had called to them. I sat there trying not to breathe fearful that they'd hear my heart pounding in my chest. They were in a little group with their heads almost together when I had a panicked thought. What if Thunderfoot shot them all in one shot?

Then they started moving toward us again. They were ten yards away. Then they were eight yards away. Now they were six yards away. I could see their eyes blinking. Why wasn't Thunderfoot shooting? "Shoot!!!!!" I whispered.

Thunderfoot touched off the ten-gauge and all hell broke loose. One turkey went straight up in the air through the trees knocking branches and leaves down like rain. Another took off down the ridge on a full run and the third one, the unfortunate one, lay flapping his wings in the leaves on the ground.

147

Thunderfoot jumped up and dived on the bird so we wouldn't get away. There was no need for that but he wasn't taking any chances.

I sat there realizing that I was shaking like a leaf. I couldn't ever remember having a turkey that close to me before and it was pretty unnerving.

"What took you so long to shoot?" I asked as Thunderfoot picked up his trophy and grinned.

"What do you mean?"

"They were in range from the first minute we saw them. Why did you wait so long?"

"If I remember right, an old turkey hunter, an expert I think, once told me...not so long ago, mind you...that I should wait for my shot as long as they were heading my way. Do you recall something like that?"

Dang, I hated it when he did that.

Thanks, Thunderfoot.

The New Boat

"Wow, is that it?" Thunderfoot asked as he came bursting through the front door. "When are we going fishing? Can I drive it? How fast will it go?"

"Whoa, take it easy. We've got a lot of work to do on it before we take it out for a test run," I said. I hardly had finished my response when he ran to the shop for tools.

I had been fishing in some walleye tournaments for a few years and as it happens in any sport, the more you get involved in something, the more equipment you think that you need. In this case the equipment was a new boat that was much fancier and bigger than my old one. When I had begun fishing tournaments most of the other fishermen had similar rigs to mine. The standard outfit was a fifteen or sixteen foot boat with about a fifty horse motor on it. Over the years the boats had grown to eighteen feet and the motors to one hundred and fifty horses. I had an opportunity to get this rig and jumped at the chance. After all, I had to keep up to the Joneses.

Thunderfoot and I began installing all the gear. We mounted the trolling motor and two fish finders, a radio, compass and GPS unit. Fishing had become high-tech and this boat had it all. There were a lot of holes to drill and what seemed like miles of wires to feed and we spent most of the day doing it. By evening we had it pretty well finished.

"Let's take her for a test drive tomorrow," Thunderfoot said enthusiastically.

"Well, the walleyes have been biting pretty well. I want to make sure everything works before I go to a tournament, so I guess it'd be a good idea to take her for a spin." I was talking to the back of Thunderfoot's head as he was running for home to get his fishing gear.

The next day after we parked at the boat landing, I showed Thunderfoot what to do to drive the boat off the trailer. He got in and I backed the boat down the landing and into the edge of the water. When the motor was in the water he started it and grinned like a madman as he backed the boat off the trailer. I parked the truck and trailer and walked down to the river where he had pulled up to the shore. I climbed into the boat and took over the steering wheel much to his dismay. "I'm driving it first," I said.

Soon we were flying upriver. At first I was a little hesitant but soon I felt more confident and gave the motor more gas. We flew like the wind in the new boat and both of us had wide grins on our faces. Thunderfoot was hanging onto his cap to keep it from blowing off.

"This is so cool," he said over the noise of the engine. Cool was an understatement for this boat.

We got to a good fishing area and I stopped the boat. I shut off the big motor and moved up to the front pedestal seat and lowered the foot-controlled trolling motor. We began drifting and jigging for walleyes. The first drift was more or less a test run for the trolling motor so I could get used to using it. When we got downriver a little way, I pulled up the trolling motor, started the big motor and took us back upriver. This time I got a small walleye right after we stopped to fish. Thunderfoot got a fish a short time later and then got another. When we got to the lower part of the drift again I turned and said, "Why don't you drive us back up? I'll lift the trolling motor and stay up front here. Just take it slow and easy."

He had a smile a mile wide as he drove us upriver. He did a good job and soon we reached the starting point, and began another drift. This time we got two more fish. When we got to the lower end again, he drove us back upriver. After several more drifts, the fishing began to slow down so we pulled onto shore for some lunch.

We were out on the shore stretching our legs and Thunderfoot just stood there looking at the boat. "That's the most beautiful boat I've ever seen," he said. I think the boy was in love.

After lunch we made two more drifts without getting any more fish so we decided to move downriver to another area. I stowed away the trolling motor and moved back to the driver's seat. Thunderfoot looked at me questioningly before he grudgingly got up so I could sit down.

"I better drive out in the river traffic," I said. "I've had more experience." He wasn't real happy about it but I had paid a lot of money for this boat and if someone was going to put the first scratch in it, I wanted it to be me.

We went downriver to another spot and again I worked the electric, and he drove us back upriver at the end of each drift. As the day wore on we accumulated a fair number of fish so we decided to call it quits. I strapped down the trolling motor and put away all the gear. When I moved back to the driver's seat Thunderfoot sat there looking at me pleading with his eyes.

"If I let you drive will you be really careful?" I asked.

He nodded his head up and down and started the motor.

We took off and he did pretty well. After a time he nudged the throttle ahead a bit and we were moving at a pretty fast clip. I had showed him how to trim the motor and raise the front of the boat, and that increased our speed also. Soon we were going real fast and I shot him a warning glance. He looked back with a look of supreme confidence. I hung on and gritted my teeth.

We were going up the channel and ahead of us was a pontoon boat that was cruising along much slower than we were. Thunderfoot looked over at me questioningly and I yelled over the noise of the motor to pass him just like you do in a car, on the left. He nodded that he understood. Instead of swinging out to the left, he kept going right at the back of the now increasingly close pontoon. In a couple more seconds we were right behind it and began wallowing in the wake of the big flat boat. The man driving the pontoon saw us overtaking him and began waving with his arms to get us to turn off. Thunderfoot tried to turn to the left but the wake of the pontoon was very large and kept pushing us back behind it. I yelled at Thunderfoot to give the motor throttle so we could jump the pontoon's wake and he finally understood and turned hard to the left as he punched the throttle. We managed to jump the wake and went around the pontoon.

As soon as we got past, I signaled to Thunderfoot to cut the motor. The man on the pontoon slumped down in his seat and shook his head as he went past us. I let out a long breath and looked over at Thunderfoot who was looking like a swim might be safer than waiting to hear what I was going to say.

"I thought you understood to pass him on the left," I said. "I don't recall telling you to drive up on his transom."

"You said to pass him like in a car. I thought you meant get right behind him and then pass. I didn't know he'd be making such a big wave. You're just lucky I'm such a good driver of we might have had a terrible accident."

Despite my near heart attack, I had to laugh. I signaled him with my thumb that he was "out" of the driver's seat. "I'll drive the rest of the way," I said. "I can't stand another close call like that today."

When we got back to the landing I backed the trailer into the water and he did a good job of driving the boat up onto it. We tied everything down and took off down the road for home.

"Boy, that's a cool boat," he said. "I sure would've felt bad if I would've crashed it. But I had it under control... really."

Even though I had been terrified, I had to grin.

"You know that guy on the pontoon?" he said. "He kind of distracted me when he was waving at me." Then he laughed. "I bet he had to go home and put on some new shorts.'

Me too.

Thanks, Thunderfoot.

Almost Too Hot to Fish

I was dozing in my recliner which I had moved to the center of the room positioning it directly under the ceiling fan. The air conditioning was running full tilt and the ceiling fan was on high and it was still warm in the house. The front door burst open and Thunderfoot came running into the house.

"Jeez, I almost melted coming from my house to here," he said. He opened the refrigerator and fanned himself with the cool air coming from it, while grabbing a cold pop. "It's nice in here. Oh, were you sleeping?"

"Well, I was but I'm not now," I said stretching to get the kinks out of my back.

We were into our third week of 100-degree weather. It was one of the longest hot spells we had ever had. I had become a hermit, content to read and sit in the air-conditioning during the day. I did some work in the evening when it cooled down to the mid-eighties. Thunderfoot who wasn't much into reading, had watched all the fishing and hunting videos I owned at least three times and was getting restless. He pestered me to go fishing every day and the longer the heat wave went on, the worse it got.

"There's a nice breeze today," he said.

"More like a blast furnace," I replied.

"Oh come on, it's not that bad. I'm going nuts sitting around here. I need to fish or I might forget how. Then what would we do?"

"What do you mean forget how?" I said. "You never knew much in the first place."

"Oh ha ha, you really crack me up! Let's go down to the river. If we get hot we can go swimming. I can't stand this anymore, please, please, please."

I almost suggested that he go home and pester his family but I had to admit that I too was getting cabin fever. "Ok, we'll try it," I said.

Of course we had to get some lunch ready. Thunderfoot never did anything without taking lunch along. We filled a cooler with cold pop and some fruit and then I opened the front door to go outside. When the hot humid air hit me I almost turned right around and went back into the house, but Thunderfoot was ahead of me chattering like a squirrel about how much fun we would have.

We backed the truck into the yard and loaded the johnboat into the back. Then we got out the volleyball net and poles, a couple of old sheets and some clothespins, and headed for the river.

The truck was like a furnace and we were sweating like construction workers. Lucy, my golden was panting up a storm as we got to the boat landing. Soon we were paddling the boat across the river to a sandbar.

When we got to the sandbar we beached the boat and stood up the volleyball net. Then we cut a couple of long branches from a tree and stuck them in near the volleyball net. We then pinned the sheets between the net and sticks making a kind of canopy from them, giving us some shade.

"Wow, this is as cool as air-conditioning," Thunderfoot gushed as we sat beneath the awning. "I'm such a smart guy to think of stuff like this. Sometimes I amaze myself."

I had to laugh. It had been a pretty good idea. We moved the boat over to the shady spot and got our poles out and began fishing. We were just fishing on the bottom with night crawlers and it didn't take long for Thunderfoot to get a bite and catch a small catfish. He quickly swung it over for me to take off for him, since he was shy about handling cats with their stingers.

Before long I had a bite and caught another catfish, then I caught another. We started catching catfish and sheephead about as fast as we could reel them in.

"This is more like it," Thunderfoot said, laughing as he set the hook into yet another fish. "I just hope our night crawlers last. It would be a shame to run out of bait when the fish are biting so good."

I didn't like the sound of that because it would entail someone, meaning me, going to the hot truck to get more bait. "Use them sparingly," I said. "Maybe we'll have enough."

After a couple of hours we took a break and walked a little way away from our fishing-hole and took a swim. Lucy had a great time frolicking in the water with Thunderfoot and we spent an hour in the water before returning to fish.

"Wow, the sun is shining right into our fishing spot," Thunderfoot said when we got back. Indeed, the sun had moved enough that our shade was now too far away for us to take advantage of it and we'd be fishing right in the sun. We adjusted the canopy so we could squeeze another hour or so from it and then began fishing again. I reached for the crawlers and dug through the bedding but found only bedding.

"The worms are gone," I said.

"You should've been more careful about using so many. Now you'll have to go get more I suppose. I'd be glad to do it but, of course, I can't drive," he said with a satisfied look.

I wasn't too keen on walking back up the sand to the boat landing and then driving for more worms but Thunderfoot kept pestering me to go so I gave up and started for the truck.

I was almost cooked when I got to the truck and by the time I drove to the bait shop and back I *was* cooked. I waded back out to the sandbar and walked toward our fishing spot. Soon I began to get worried as I couldn't see Thunderfoot or Lucy sitting under the canopy. I looked up and down the sandbar and they weren't anywhere to be found. Now I was getting worried because the river has a fast current and can be dangerous if you get careless.

I began to trot and then run toward the fishing spot. As I neared it I finally figured out why I hadn't seen them. Thunderfoot was sitting in the water with just his head and one hand showing, holding his pole. Lucy was sitting right beside him with just her head showing.

"It's about time, I was almost out of bait," he said grinning from the water.

"Jeez, you guys gave me a scare, I thought you must have drowned or something."

"Me drown? Me, part man part fish?" he said as he hooked another fish.

I sat down and laid the worm container in the sand when a thought struck me. "Hey, how is it that you're still fishing when we were out of bait?"

"Oh, that's a funny story," he said. "It seems that I had put a few worms into another can and forgot about them. Right after you left I happened to find them but you were already gone...but there were only a few anyway, not enough for both of us." He put on his most innocent face and sat there actually expecting me to buy this line of baloney.

"Yeah right," I said. I opened the cooler for a pop. It was empty. "What happened to all the pop and food?"

"Well, Lucy and I were pretty hungry. I guess we must have eaten it all. Maybe you should go and...oh never mind."

"Never mind is right, at least until I check and see what else you've stashed away around here."

He gave me an innocent look and then a big grin.

Thanks, Thunderfoot.

The Safari North

Thunderfoot was standing beside the pile of gear in his front yard and began picking up bags as I drove onto the driveway. We were taking a fishing trip "up north" and he was ready and waiting.

"Jeez! Where have you been?" he asked. "I've been ready for hours." He struggled to get the two duffel bags into the back of the truck.

"I'm three minutes late," I answered. "And by the way, what *is* all this stuff?"

He shot me a look of amazement. "This is all necessary stuff. The big bag is my sleeping bag, an extra blanket, pillow, air mattress and my heavy coat. The smaller bag is clothes, shoes, raingear, and mosquito stuff. The little bag is beautifying stuff, like my shampoo, soap, stink-me-pretty, and my shaving machine. The rest is fishing stuff."

"Your shaving machine? Since when do you shave?" I asked.

"My grandpa gave me his old shaving machine a couple of years ago and I shaved with it then."

"And you think you might just have to shave again while we're on vacation? What are you going to use for electricity?"

He looked at me questioningly. "What do you mean? No electricity? What am I going to use to play my Discman?"

We loaded the gear and headed up the road to the north woods. As we passed through countless towns, he announced the name and population of each. It was if I couldn't see the sign I guess. Somehow the conversation ended up being about whether the American flag decals on a Harvester silo meant it was paid for or not.

"See that one? It's got a flag so that's a rich farmer," he said every time we spotted a silo with a flag. I didn't know if it was true so I didn't argue about it.

On we went with only a couple of pit stops and soon the

countryside began to look more "northern".

"Are there any bears up here?" he asked.

"Yeah, from here on up this is bear country, but we most likely won't see one."

The words had hardly left my lips when he yelled, "Stop! Look, a bear!"

I looked to the left where he was pointing and sure enough there was a huge black bear lying along the road dead as a doornail.

"Stop, let's look at it," he said, digging for his camera.

I pulled over on the shoulder and he ran back to the bear. As he got closer he slowed to a walk and then to a stealthy walk. He stopped and watched for it to breathe and then carefully walked up to it.

It was a really big black bear and had probably been hit by a car. "I'll sit on its back and you take my picture," he said handing me the camera.

He stepped across the bear and sat down on his back, grabbed his ears and lifted up the head grinning like a madman and I snapped a picture.

"Boy, just wait till the guys at school see that," he said grinning from ear to ear.

We started off down the road again and soon crossed the border into Michigan. We came to a town a short while later and he didn't read the name and population. Instead he had a puzzled look on his face. Down the road a few miles the same thing happened.

"Where do the people go when the limit is filled?" he asked.

"What limit? What do you mean?" I replied.

"Well, both of those last towns said the name and city limit. I guess that means they have all the people they want. They must have a limit. What do the people who want to live here do? Wait till somebody moves out?"

I started laughing and he looked even more confused. "City limit is the edge of the city's jurisdiction," I explained. "It's the edge of the city, not the population limit. They don't population figures on signs in Michigan I guess."

"Oh." He looked kind of embarrassed.

Before long we arrived at the town on the edge of the national forest campground that was our destination. We stopped at a bait shop and got licenses and some information from an old-timer who was sitting behind the counter.

"Any bears in this campground?" Thunderfoot asked.

"Bears? You betcha! They's thick around here. Why just last week they carried off a couple of college kids."

Thunderfoot's eyes got real big.

"The state-record bear was shot up the road a piece," the old-timer continued. "He was so big it took a log skidder to get him out of the woods. But usually they don't bother campers too much. Once in a while they might chomp somebody but not too often. Just be sure to keep your food in the truck and you'll most likely come back alive."

The old guy winked at me while Thunderfoot was deep in thought.

"Which lake you boys goin to?"

"White Goose Lake," I said.

"Uh-oh. That's the one nearest where that giant bear was killed. He probably has some giant kids that are all grown up by now, I'd be plenty careful up there."

Thunderfoot was very quiet taking it all in. "You want to take a few candy bars with us?" I asked.

He shook his head no. "It's your last chance for snacks," I warned.

He declined again, so we packed into the truck and started down the highway until we came to a forest road that led to the lake. The road was a rocky track that snaked through the trees and in some places it was so narrow that we couldn't have opened the truck doors if we had wanted to get out. We drove for what seemed like many miles and then suddenly we came over a little rise and there was the lake. It was very pretty with a tree-lined shoreline and a pit toilet with a hand pumped well. There wasn't another tent or camper to be seen.

"The bears probably ate all the other people who were here," Thunderfoot concluded matter-of-factly.

"Oh don't worry," I said. "That old guy was just having fun with you. Chances are that neither of us will get eaten."

It was pretty late in the afternoon so we decided to get the tent set up and the camp ready rather than go fishing. It took the better part of a couple of hours but when we were done we had a dandy little campsite. I lit a fire in our fire pit and after it died down a little we grilled some hamburgers, ate some chips and drank a couple of pops. Soon it was time for bed. Thunderfoot searched the campsite for any scrap of food and made sure all the coolers were locked in the truck. Then he came into the tent.

"There's nothing edible in here but us," he said.

"Quit worrying. We'll be fine."

We rolled out our sleeping bags onto our cots and climbed in. I lay on my back and listened to the sounds of the night. I loved the sounds near a lake. There were frogs croaking, some cicadas singing and an occasional owl hooting. It was very peaceful and soon the sounds were joined by the gently deep breathing of my young friend. I rolled over on my side and was just about to sleep when I heard the sound of a loon echoing across the lake.

To those who have never heard a loon, it's a pretty scary sound. Their call starts out with a low wailing sound that increases in volume and pitch as it goes on. The moaning sound ends up with a high pitched whistling sound that is quite un-nerving if you don't know what it is.

Thunderfoot had never heard a loon before.

"What the heck was that?" I heard him ask from deep in his sleeping bag. He had pulled the bag up over his head and he was crunched down inside. The loon call came again and he peeked out of the opening. "Did you hear that? Hey, are you awake?"

I began to laugh. "It's only a loon," I said.

'A what?"

"A loon...you know...those big black and white birds that cruise on the water up here."

"Are you sure?"

"Yup."

Out came his head. "Jeez, I almost had the big one. I thought it was a bear screaming at me and coming to eat me. You're sure that's a bird?"

The sound came again. "Yeah, it's a loon. If we go down by the lake I bet we'll see him in the moonlight."

"As interesting as that sounds, I think I'll just stay here in my sleeping bag," he said.

"Suit yourself. I'm going to go see if I can spot him."

"Are you nuts? You'd leave me here alone? I'll make a deal with you. You stay here and I'll do all the chores all week. All you have to do is relax."

"Well, I'd really like to see that loon."

"I'll clean all the fish too."

"Ok, I'll stay," I said.

"Good, now go to sleep."

This was looking like a real good vacation.

Thanks Thunderfoot.

Right Place, Wrong Time

The north wind bit into our faces as we hunkered down in our duck blind, straining to see any moving ducks through the morning darkness. It was late in the season and Thunderfoot and I had gotten to the blind early so we could replace some of the teal and wood duck decoys with large mallards and goose decoys. This would be one of our last hunts of the season.

"Jeez, I'm just about froze," he grumbled from somewhere inside his hunting coat. He had the thing zipped up so far that only the top of his head was showing. "How long is it until we can shoot?"

I checked my watch. Shooting time has just started but with the cloudy skies and cold wind it was hard to see anything that might be close enough to shoot at.

"It's time right now," I said.

Thunderfoot's head poked out of his collar and he got ready for some shooting. Before long we saw a flock of mallards flying up the river and I called to them. They kept right on going, showing no interest in us.

Suddenly Thunderfoot grabbed my arm and whispered, "Listen...geese."

I strained my ears and soon heard the unmistakable barking call of Canada geese coming from our right. We looked and looked but couldn't see them even though their calls were obviously getting closer. Finally Thunderfoot whispered, "Look, they're real low over the lake."

Sure enough, the geese were just above the water of the lake just east of us. We hunted on a small beaver pond west of the lake which was about a quarter of a mile away. The lake took a dog-leg at the west end and the flock followed that dog-leg and settled into the narrow arm of water. Soon another flock followed the same route and settled down with the first bunch.

"We should have been over there," Thunderfoot said.

"Yeah, and if we were they would have landed here," I answered.

"Maybe we should pick up our decoys and go over there."

We had one dozen Canada goose decoys sitting on the pond but I wasn't real enthused about picking them all up and then carrying everything over to the lake. Thunderfoot kept pestering me and then another flock of geese landed in the same dog-leg and that sealed it. We began the big move.

I took the canoe out to the pond and wrapped the cords around the necks of the decoys while Thunderfoot carried the guns, ammo, and seat cushions back to high ground. Then we carried the decoys up the high bank and walked through the woods a short was and started toward the lake. Of course when we got close to the lake the geese got up and flew away, but we expected that. There was some reason geese were landing in the dog-leg and we figured if we put our decoys there we might just get some shooting.

The whole process took almost two hours and during that time four more flocks of geese came down the marsh and followed pretty much the same course.

This is going to be great," Thunderfoot said as we finished putting out the decoys. "It's lucky the lake is shallow here or you'd have had to get wet to put out the decoys." How thoughtful of him.

While I had been placing the decoys Thunderfoot constructed a makeshift blind out of cattails and buttonball brush ad the edge of the lake.

We settled in and felt sure we were now in the right place for some action. We waited. We waited some more. An hour later we were still waiting. Not one goose had shown his face on the marsh since we had moved. Another hour passed. The clouds began to dissipate and the sun came out. It turned into a bluebird day and not one goose came near us.

"I can't believe it," Thunderfoot said. "Now it's a nice day and the ducks and geese will be flying way too high and we're gonna sit here all day and shoot nothing." He lay back in the tall grass and folded his arms across his chest.

"Well, at least it warmed up," I said trying to cheer him up. I dug into our lunch bag and offered him a sandwich, which seemed to boost his moral a little. In the hours that followed we sat there and enjoyed a beautiful afternoon but saw no ducks or geese.

By mid-afternoon we were getting pretty bored and still hoped that the evening flight would be better. We had seen a lot of birds in the morning, so hopefully some of them would come past again towards evening.

"I think I'll go over there and cut some of that tall grass to make us a better blind," he said. He stood up and began walking toward the marsh. "That way if they do come back we'll be hidden better."

I was ready for as stretch too, so I went along with him. We cut some grass with our hunting knives and carried it back to the lake. We needed a bit more so we walked back and were cutting it when I heard the first honk. Thunderfoot stopped in mid-cut and gave me a panicked look.

"Did you hear that?" he whispered. I nodded and we turned slowly toward the lake. Hovering above our decoys about ten feet off the water were fifteen geese. A couple of seconds later they landed in among our decoys.

"Our guns! We left our guns over there!" Thunderfoot was having a meltdown.

I knew it was futile but I said. "Let's get down and belly-crawl over and see if we can get to the guns before the geese see us."

We low-crawled as fast as we could go, and got within ten feet of the guns when the geese began honking and lifted off the water. By the time we grabbed our guns they were safely out of range.

"Sure, go!" he yelled at the geese. "I can't believe we did that. I can't believe we left our guns behind!"

As exasperated as I was I had to laugh. Soon Thunderfoot was laughing too. "Can you believe we did that?" he said shaking his head. "I thought you taught me better than that."

We settled back down in our now much improved blind and didn't see a waterfowl of any kind the rest of the afternoon. The time ticked by and soon it was time go home.

"Not one goose came by here all afternoon except those that came while we were over there," he said. "What are the odds of that happening?"

"With us? Pretty good," I said.

We picked up the decoys and began hauling all the stuff back toward the high bank and about half way back we heard geese honking. We stopped and watched as a flock of about twenty landed right in the dog-leg where our blind was built. "Well that's about it," he said shaking his head.

I grinned. "Look at it this way. We got to spend a beautiful day in the outdoors and now we don't have to spend an hour picking geese."

He nodded. "So, what's the plan for tomorrow?"

At least the boy wasn't a quitter.

Thanks, Thunderfoot.

The Great Coyote Hunt

"I'm just about to climb the walls," Thunderfoot said, pacing back and forth across the living room. "We've been cooped up like this for weeks. There's got to be something we can do outside."

It had been one of those winters. January had been as bitter cold as Siberia. The thermometer hadn't been higher than ten degrees above zero for almost three weeks. It was beginning to drive everyone crazy.....especially Thunderfoot. The fishing had been at an all time low due to the cold and the high pressure fronts that came through every other day. The last few times we had gone we'd caught nothing.

I was trying to read a magazine but he kept pacing around like a caged animal.

"Here," I said tossing him the magazine. "This is a new magazine...look through it and see if you can entertain yourself while I get us something to eat.

He grabbed the magazine and I went into the kitchen to see what there was to eat. It seemed like food usually improved his mood. When I came back to the living room he was intently reading an article in the magazine. I put his food down next to him but he kept reading and ignored the food. That *must* have been a good article.

"We have a lot of coyotes around here don't we?" he asked.

"Yeah, I guess so. They say there are a lot of them but you don't see them very often because they're so stealthy."

"This story tells about calling them in so you can shoot them. It tells how to camouflage yourself and call and how to get them to come to you. It sounds like fun. I think we should try it."

I read the article and while he devoured both his snack and mine. When I finished he looked at me and grinned. "Well, what do you think? Let's try hunting for them we've done stupider things than this."

I laughed and couldn't argue with that. And so we began our preparations for the great coyote hunt.

First we needed sheets to use as camouflage. We found some old ones in the closet that were about worn out so we cut holes in them so we could wear them over our clothes like a poncho. Then we got some plastic sheeting to lay on the ground and an old sleeping bag to lay over the sheeting to keep the cold from seeping into us. Finally we found some old pillow cases that we could wear over our hats and faces. We cut eyeholes in them and tried them on.

"Yikes, we look like Ku Kluxers," Thunderfoot said. "We better wait until we get where we're going before we put them on."

Next we went to buy a coyote call. Of course there aren't just a couple of calls for coyotes. There are dozens of different models that make many different sounds. Some sound like a mouse squeaking and others sound like a dying rabbit. One mimicked a coyote bark. We finally decided on a dying rabbit and when we got outside Thunderfoot gave it a try.

The wailing sound was as spooky as heck. "Wow," he said, "I'd hate to hear that on a dark and stormy night."

It was getting late in the day, so we decided to start our hunt first thing the next morning. As is usually the case when we're going hunting, Thunderfoot stayed over in "his" room. It saved me waking him up and the rest of his family at the same time.

At dawn we got up and had a big breakfast and then drove down to the river bottoms looking for a good coyote spot. We found a place that looked just right. It was near the marsh and a little higher than the surrounding terrain so it had a good view of the prairie near a pine woods. There was a lot of cover but many open areas so we'd be able to see a coyote if he came close.

We unloaded the gear and I drove the truck about a quarter of a mile down the road and parked it. I walked back and we carried the gear to the little knoll. It was pretty brushy but looked like a really good spot.

First we cleared off a small area and laid the plastic down.

Then we put down the sleeping bag and spread a sheet over it. Next we got out our sheets and hoods and covered up. Finally we lay down on the sleeping bag and Thunderfoot loaded the gun. We had lunch, of course, and we covered it with another pillow case. We blended in and looked like a little bump in the snow.

"We're camouflaged so good that nothing can see us," he said as he dug into his pocket for the dying-rabbit call. He put it in his mouth and produced a horrifying call that would have given shivers to an undertaker. We scanned the area, expecting a coyote to come bounding up at any second, but none came. After a while Thunderfoot wailed on the call again and then again. We waited and waited but we saw no coyotes.

"That article said they should come on the run," Thunderfoot said.

"Well, those articles sometimes tell it like we want it to be, not like it is," I said. "We've got all day, so just be patient."

But it was cold and it wasn't getting any warmer. At first we were pretty comfortable but as we lay there the cold began to creep in.

"We should have brought a blanket or sleeping bag to put on top of us too," Thunderfoot said. I nodded in agreement. Then he put the call in his mouth and blew. "Ummmffe".

When I looked over he had the call in his mouth but it was frozen shut. Now it was also frozen to his lips. He had a panicked look on his face.

"Nice calling," I said laughing. "That should bring them in running."

He didn't think I was very funny. "Put your hands around the call and blow on it, so it'll thaw out," I said.

He cupped his hands around the call and huffed and puffed and before long the call slipped from his lips.

"Holy cow, I never thought it was *that* cold. Here, you call from now on."

I slipped the call inside my coat and it quickly thawed out.

168

Then I blew a long mournful note on it.

It was getting colder and colder and I looked at my watch. We had been there two hours already without seeing a thing.

"What do you think?" I asked. "Maybe we should try it another time. There don't seem to be any coyotes around here."

Thunderfoot looked at me with chattering teeth. "Yeah, I think...Wait! Look!"

I turned and way off at the edge of the trees was a coyote standing there looking out over the prairie.

I dug furiously for the call and gave it a short blow, trying to let the coyote know where the dying rabbit was located. Sure enough he began trotting toward us.

"Jeez, he's coming," Thunderfoot said, slowly moving his gun into shooting position. The coyote was still coming our way slowly but surely. I called again. He stopped and looked right at us. We froze and didn't move a muscle.

There was a little dip in the terrain and the coyote dropped into it and out of our sight for a minute.

"Where did he go?" Thunderfoot whispered.

"I think he's still coming. Just be real still and quiet."

Time seemed to stand still. We lay there shivering waiting for the coyote to reappear. Suddenly like a ghost there he was. He stood only twenty yards from us.

"There he is," I whispered. Thunderfoot nodded and thumbed off the safety.

The coyote stood looking our way staring hard, looking for the rabbit. I didn't dare move or try to call again.

Suddenly he acted like he got a whiff of our scent and he whirled and disappeared back into the swale. Then we saw him trotting back into the woods.

I looked at Thunderfoot who took off his hood and gave ma an amazed look.

"I didn't know how much they look like dogs," he said. "I just couldn't shoot it."

I patted him on the back. "No problem pal," I said. "We did

169

what we set out to do. We called him in and fooled him...whether or not we killed him doesn't matter. We had the fun of fooling a wild critter into thinking we were dinner."

He looked at me and grinned. "I thought you might be mad that I didn't shoot."

"You should know by now that something like that wouldn't bother me," I said. "Did you wonder why I gave you the gun? I didn't want to shoot a coyote in the first place."

We stood up and stretched the kinks out of our backs. "I think I've had enough fresh air for one day," I said.

"Me too," he answered. "Boy this cold air makes me hungry."

Somehow I knew he was going to say that.

Thanks, Thunderfoot.

How About a Little Help Here?

I was sitting in the back yard enjoying the shade on one of those hot, humid days when even the thought of movement made me start to sweat. The western sky was filling with big high fluffy white clouds that would soon begin to turn black and threatening. There would be a storm before the day was out.

I knew it wouldn't be long before Thunderfoot would run over from his house and want to go fishing. It never failed. On the hottest days of the year he always thought we should go fishing. Of course, he was right. Northerns and bass become very active right before a storm hits and many times in the past we had seen fabulous fishing on days just like this one.

Right on cue, I saw Thunderfoot heading across the yard. He was marching along...a man on a mission.

"You're not going to catch any fish sitting here in the shade," he said as he plopped down in the lawn chair next to me.

"Yeah, but I'm also not going to die of heat-stroke by going out in the sun either," I replied.

"Yeah, I know you old guys can't take the heat. When you begin to get feeble, it's hard on you. That's ok. I just thought it looked like a nice evening to go fishing, but never mind.....I'll just stay home, or I could ride my bike down to the river and fish off the bank. You know down by the boat landing...it's not good fishing but it's better than nothing at all." He sat there looking miserable, kind of like Oliver Twist asking for more porridge...the poor pathetic little thing.

"Get the stuff," I said. I was so easy.

We loaded the johnboat and the gear into the back of the pickup. When we arrived at the lake we slid the boat into the water and I drove the pickup to the parking area. By the time I had walked back to the boat landing Thunderfoot had distributed the gear to the proper ends of the boat and was sharpening the hook of a new lure he had bought.

"This is going to be a killer," he said proudly showing off a plastic frog.

"That looks good," I said. "I'm surprised that you knew where to *buy* lures. I thought you figured they all came free from my tackle box." He looked up innocently and kept sharpening.

"I'll have you know..." he began.

"Just get in the boat," I said as I began pushing off.

As we moved away from the shore, Thunderfoot cast his new frog lure into the lily pads and then began making it crawl slowly across the tops of the plants. The plastic frog hadn't gone two feet when the lily pads exploded and a nice bass engulfed his lure. He fought it expertly and soon had it alongside the boat. As he lifted the fish he grinned like a maniac. He didn't say a word, but unhooked the fish and released it, grinning slyly all the while. He reeled up and cast to another spot in the weeds. This time he reeled the lure back without a strike but got another bass on the next cast.

Meanwhile I paddled the boat and cast to the weeds with different baits that I thought might produce a fish for me. But I had no bites. Thunderfoot sat in the front of the boat, casting and catching fish like a machine.

"What do you think of my frog now?" he asked.

"I think you should have bought two...one for me too," I said glumly with sweat running into my eyes.

"Well, it just so happens that I have another just like this one...here in my pocket," he said reaching into his shorts pocket and producing another frog lure. "If someone would like to use it I might be able to let them if they ask real nice."

I wiped the sweat from my eyes and gave him a hard look. "If you'd like to swim back to shore, keep that frog, otherwise toss it over here."

"Sounds like a plan to me," he said grinning as he tossed the precious lure back to me.

"How many fish were you going to catch before you let me have this extra bait?" I asked.

"I completely forgot I had it in my pocket until you asked," he said innocently.

Well, it didn't really make much difference because now I had a frog and soon we both began catching fish, one after another. We caught northerns, bass, dogfish and Thunderfoot even caught a huge crappie that was 16 inches long. As much as I hated to admit it, the fishing had turned out as good as he had predicted it would be just before a storm.

We were near a little island with a couple of trees on it when Thunderfoot cast toward the spot and his frog ended up in one of the trees. He pulled and pulled and suddenly his line snapped. "Holy cow, I lost my frog. I might need that one I lent to you back."

"I'll take you over to the island. You can climb that tree and get yours back," I said.

He seemed ok with that so I paddled over and he climbed out and walked to the tree. Up he went and soon he was shimmying out onto the branch that held his frog. He broke off the branch holding the frog and then climbed back down from the tree. He tossed the bait into the boat and began walking back towards me when he suddenly stopped and grabbed something in the grass. I watched as he tugged and pulled on something that was hidden by the tall grass.

"Come here and help me," he said.

"What are you doing?"

"I need help. Come here."

I wasn't real sure I wanted to get too close to whatever he was doing but I stepped out onto the island and carefully made my way to where he was crouching in the grass. When I got to him I stepped back quickly as soon as I saw what he was doing. He was holding onto the tail of a huge snake that was partly in a hole in the ground. He was tugging on the tail trying to pull the dang thing out of the hole.

"Are you crazy?" I said retreating back to the boat as fast as I could go. "Let that thing go and get back into the boat or I'm

173

leaving you here." My patience with snakes was zero.

"I thought you might like to see this nice snake," he said laughing. Suddenly he fell over backward holding onto about six inches of the snake's tail.

"Goodbye," I said backing the boat away.

"Oops, I didn't mean to do that."

As he spoke, a huge water snake came to the surface right by the boat. The snake was obviously not in a good mood. It swam by my end of the boat and I could see that its rear end was kind of blunt. It didn't even slow down as it passed, heading for the other side of the lake.

"Come back and get me...please," Thunderfoot begged.

"Not until you get rid of that snake tail." I knew that if he got in the boat with it, it would somehow end up in my lap.

He grinned and tossed the tail, so I picked him up.

"You're pretty sensitive about snakes," he said grinning.

"You're darn right and the sooner you learn that the better off you'll be," I said.

"Sorry, I was just having fun."

We fished in silence for a while and soon began catching fish again. We worked our way back to the landing because the thunderstorm was getting close. We wanted to be off the water before the lightning began to strike.

"What did you think of my frog baits?" Thunderfoot asked as we loaded the boat.

"Not bad," I replied.

"I think I'll get a couple more just in case we lose one next time. Then we won't have to go up on the bank and risk a venomous encounter with a killer grass snake." He grinned at me. "I wouldn't want my best boat-rower to have a heart attack."

He was such a considerate boy.

Thanks, Thunderfoot.

The High-Rise

I looked up from my book to see Thunderfoot coming across the yard with a bow in his hand. He was grinning from ear to ear as he walked up and held the bow out for my inspection.

"I just got it today. I've been saving up all summer," he said proudly as he handed me the new compound bow.

It was a fine bow, but it lacked all of the extra equipment, like a sight, an arrow rest, a peep, and silencers for the string.

"It's missing some stuff," I said.

"Well, I thought maybe I could borrow some of the stuff off your old bow since you don't shoot much anymore. When I get more money saved up, I'll buy my own stuff and put yours back on your bow," he said nodding his head.

I had once bought a bow and practiced all summer with it. I had become a pretty good shot, but I retired from bow hunting after spending only one day in the woods. My problem was that in bow hunting, you have to be real close to the deer....and when I got that close, I just couldn't shoot it. The encounter became too personal, I guess, and I didn't have the heart to let the arrow go. So, I put my bow up on the wall and there it still was hanging. Thunderfoot had wanted to use it but the draw was much too long for him, so he had to get his own bow. However, my accessories would work for him.

"Those things aren't doing anyone any good hanging on the garage wall, so you might as well take them and keep them," I said. "I don't need them anyway."

"Cool!" He was off to the garage to strip down my bow. I went back to my book. He came back a while later with his bow fitted with all the gear that was necessary to make it work.

"This is awesome. Oh, by the way, could I borrow some of that scrap lumber you've got stacked in the garage? Then I can make a little shooting platform in my tree."

"Sure," I said. "Learning to shoot from a tree is a good idea."

Later, I headed back into the house for the evening. I could hear the sound of a power saw and hammering coming from Thunderfoot's back yard as he constructed his shooting platform. The next day I was out of town. I drove past Thunderfoot's house on my way back home.

I could see it from a block away. His shooting platform looked like a small cabin suspended in the tree in his back yard. It was about twenty feet up in the tree, and he had built a ladder going up to it. The platform itself was about six feet square, with side rails and a sloping roof above it.

Thunderfoot was up in the cabin, waving at me to come and look. "Come on up here!" he hollered. "The view is great."

"No way...I'm not climbing up in that thing," I said. "It's a bit more than I expected to see. What I had in mind was something like a tree stand, not a building. Do I have any lumber leftover?

He looked sheepish. "Well, not much. I kind of got carried away, but it sure turned out good, huh?"

I had to laugh in spite of the fact that he had used up all my boards. "What does your mom think?" I asked.

"She's not too thrilled, but I think she'll get used to it. Want to see how it works?"

He nocked an arrow into his bow and took aim at a bunch of cardboard strapped together by the back fence. He shot the arrow into a black spot he had drawn on the cardboard. "What do you think of that?"

I was impressed and told him so, then took off for home. As I sat in my kitchen, I could see Thunderfoot up in his tree. He would shoot at the cardboard target, and climb down to retrieve his arrows. Then head back up the tree for another round. I called the local archery shop and after talking with the owner for a few minutes, I drove over to the shop.

When I got there he was just putting practice tips on a dozen new arrows. He had also put all the extra parts onto a new life-sized foam deer target.

"This will make your friend pretty happy," he said as I paid for the items.

"Yeah, I think he'll be pretty surprised," I said.

That night I waited until all the lights went out at Thunderfoot's house. Then I quietly walked over with the deer target and the arrows. I stood the target in front of the pile of cardboard, laid the new arrows on top of the target, and snuck home.

The next morning the phone rang at a few minutes to seven. It was Thunderfoot. "I can't believe you did that! Jeez, you're the best!"

"What are you talking about? I said still half asleep.

"The target and the arrows! I know you did that, didn't you?"

I was finally awake. "Oh, yeah, I thought you might have more fun shooting at something that looked more real. And with more arrows, you won't have to climb up and down so many times."

"Thanks a million."

"No problem, have fun with them."

The next few weeks passed with Thunderfoot shooting hundreds of arrows into the target. He went up and down the tree ladder dozens of times and just about wore out the target. He moved it from place to place and practiced at different distances until he could hit it in the vital areas with each shot.

He called me one evening close to the opening of the deer season and invited me over for a demonstration. He climbed his tree and put all twelve arrows I into the target in precisely the places he wanted. I was impressed. He was a good shot, and he could easily kill any deer that came into range.

"Well, what do you think?" he asked.

"Impressive," I said. "I guess the practice did the trick."

"I'm going up on my uncle's farm on Saturday. He's got a tree stand for me to hunt from, and he said there's a big buck in that woods.

I wished him luck and went home.

Saturday was a beautiful day. The sun came up on one of

those perfect fall days. The temperature was perfect the sky was sunny with a slight breeze. You couldn't have asked for a better day for the opening of archery season. I worked in the garden and around the house and my thoughts were often of my young buddy. I imagined him sitting in the three with his new bow waiting for the big buck to come along.

Late in the afternoon, I saw his uncle's truck pulling out from Thunderfoot's driveway, so I knew he was home. A short time later he came walking toward my house. I could tell by his walk that he hadn't had any luck.

"No deer?" I asked.

He gave a big sigh and sat down in a lawn chair.

"You know how you quit bow hunting because you couldn't shoot one? Well, now I know what you mean. I had a big buck come right up to my spot. I pulled the bow back and he looked up at me, and I just stood there until finally he walked away. I couldn't shoot him."

"It's a lot different when you're looking them in the eye isn't it? I asked.

He nodded. "Boy, you got that right. Shooting them with a gun is kind of impersonal, but with a bow they're too close. You can see them way too good. I guess I wasted a lot of time and money."

"No," I said. "You didn't waste anything. You can still shoot at targets, and you've become very proficient with a bow. You didn't waste anything."

He smiled at me. "I've got my tree house now too. Maybe I can put sides on it and make it a real tree house. Then just in case mom kicks me out someday, I'll have a place to stay. You got any more lumber?"

Thanks, Thunderfoot.

You Chase...I'll Shoot

Thunderfoot and I drove up past the barn and parked the pickup at the edge of the field. We were at the end of a long valley with hay fields along the edges and picked corn up the middle. The valley was guarded by steep hills on both sides, and our host had given us directions the previous evening as to where the best spot would be to get a deer.

We had not had too successful a season so far, and Thunderfoot was a bit on the grumpy side. During opening day and Sunday of the first weekend, we had sat on stands along the river bottoms and had seen absolutely nothing to shoot at. School forced Thunderfoot to give it a rest for the next three days and now we were back at it on Thanksgiving morning.

"We'll see some deer here," I said. "Ken said there are lots of does and some nice bucks still roaming around." The owner and his family had filled all of their buck tags on the previous weekend and wanted some does taken off the farm, so things looked good for us.

Thunderfoot was still down. He wasn't the patient type. He liked a lot of action and the previous two days of fruitless hunting were about enough to make him have a fit.

"Well, we can't do any worse than that last 'hot spot' you took me to," he said gloomily.

I didn't answer him, but opened my door quietly and reached back into the pickup for my gun and my other gear. He also got out of the truck and we got prepared to move up the valley in the darkness.

"Ken said to go up the side valley by the old windmill," I whispered as we walked slowly along the fence.

We soon saw the windmill and crossed the fence a short way from it. I saw a nice stump up on the side of the nearby hill and told Thunderfoot to sit there. I would go back and climb up the hill on the other side of the point, where I could hopefully chase some deer to him.

179

"I'll start up the hill in about an hour," I said. "You just watch from here. If I move any, they should come right through here."

He nodded, and I walked back toward the point of the hill so I could go up the next valley and ascend the hill from the other side.

When I got to the back side of the hill, it was still way too dark for an old man with bad knees to start climbing, so I sat down on a log and rested for a while.

Blackness turned to gray, and my eyes and ears were soon imagining critters all around me in the woods. Stumps seemed to make small movements, like a deer standing and watching you might make. A stick or an acorn falling to the ground sounded like a footstep on the dry leaves. But as the light got stronger, the stumps became what they really were and the footsteps became acorns and sticks that fell naturally all day long. It's funny how your eyes and ears can play mind tricks on you when you're in a dark woods.

As it got light I looked up at the hillside I planned to climb. It was much steeper than I expected. In fact it was real steep, and the top was a long, long way from me. "Oh boy, what have I gotten myself into?" I thought.

I started up the hill and at first I followed a deer path. Soon the deer path became too steep for me to follow and I had to abandon it. Then I worked my way from tree to tree and rock to rock trying not to make too much noise and trying not to slip and slide all the way to the bottom of the hill. I hated the idea of having to re-conquer land that I had already once trod over.

It didn't take long for me to work up a sweat. Soon I was huffing and puffing like a steam engine. I would move up a few feet and then hang onto a tree for a few minutes to let my heart rate go down again. Then I'd move up another few feet. It was slow going and suddenly I looked up and saw a small bunch of deer up the hill from me. They were casually waking away from Thunderfoot's direction.

I would gain ten or fifteen feet, rest, and then climb some

more. The top of the hill seemed to stay the same distance away. Just as I was beginning to think I would never reach the top I heard a shot, followed about ten seconds later by another shot.

I stood there panting and listened. No more shots, no shouts, nothing came from the other side of the hill. Now I had to make a decision. Should I keep going up or should I go back to see if Thunderfoot was the shooter and had he shot a deer? Since I was already halfway up the hill, I decided I should go the rest of the way and finish out my drive. I waited another ten minutes and didn't hear a thing.

So, I started on up to the top of the hill. Once on high ground, I always hate to go back down unless I have to. High ground is gained at too high a price for a "seasoned hunter", as Thunderfoot called me. Of course I knew he was saying "Old Man."

I kept working my way to the top and finally made it. It was a beautiful spot. The ridge top was flat and dozens of deer trails crisscrossed it. I found a dandy stump and sat on it with my back against a nice flat tree trunk, resting.

"I think I'll sit here for half and hour or so and see what comes by," I thought to myself.

I was very comfortable and then I heard a "hey" coming from the bottom of the hill. I listened and heard it again. Thunderfoot.

I didn't really want to yell back, because I had just settled into my comfortable seat, but thought I'd better answer him in case he had trouble. "What?" I yelled back.

"Come down."

"Did you get one?"

"Come down."

"Do you have a deer?"

"Just come down."

I grudgingly picked up my gear and started down the face of the hill. I tried to go slow and pick my way down but soon I had to almost run to stay upright. The front of the hill was as steep as the back had been. Soon I was panting and sweating again from my "controlled fall" down the hill.

I finally saw Thunderfoot sitting on a stump at the bottom of the hill, so I stopped.

"Did you get one?"

"Two."

"What?"

"Two."

That was great news. He had a Hunter's Choice tag and I had a buck tag, so he had filled both of them.

He was all grins and swagger as I got to him.

"How big is he? Where is he?" I asked.

"He who? I got two does."

I looked at him. "Two does? We don't have two doe permits, just one."

His mouth dropped open. "I thought you had a Hunter's Choice too."

"No, I've just got my regular buck tag. Why did you shoot two?"

"Well, three came over that little knoll over there and I shot and they all ran away. But pretty soon two of them came back over the little knoll again. I shot again and they ran away again, and when I walked over there, two of them were lying there."

We walked across the valley and sure enough, there were two nice does lying side by side.

Thunderfoot was getting worried, so I told him that Ken had mentioned that they had several doe tags left and if we got an extra one, they'd take it. He brightened up when he heard that.

"It's not exactly the way it should be done, but we won't leave a deer go to waste over some little rule infraction. It'll all work out fine," I said.

"Well, it makes me feel better about climbing that mountain since you got these deer for all my effort," I said.

He gave me a funny look. "Those deer came from the other side of the valley. I don't think you chased them, but it was a nice idea anyway."

I had climbed that monster hill for nothing.

"I'd like to try field dressing them, but I think I want to watch you one or two more times, just to see how an expert does it," Thunderfoot said.

Why not? I might as well do something right.

Thanks, Thunderfoot.

Go Toward the Light

It was a clear cold January day and I was nice and cozy in my recliner when Thunderfoot came through the front door. He stomped the snow from his boots and stood grinning at me. He was dressed for hunting so I knew what to expect.

"My grandpa wants me to take his beagle out and hunt him for a while. What do you think?"

"Your grandpa asked you to take his dog hunting?"

"Yeah...well, I was talking to him on the phone and it kind of came up. He said the dog was restless and could use some exercise so I told him we would be glad to help out."

I couldn't argue with logic like that, so I dressed in my hunting clothes and grabbed a shotgun and some shells. Meanwhile Thunderfoot rummaged through the refrigerator looking for some 'pocket food' to take along.

We drove to grandpa's farm and picked up Pat, the three-year old beagle who needed to be taken hunting. Grandpa was content to let us crawl through the snow by ourselves. He gave us some ideas as to where to go, we headed to the woods.

We started up a long valley and it wasn't too long before Pat picked up the track of a rabbit and took off, howling like a fire siren. We separated and waited. In just a little while a bunny came hopping through the brush. He was just out of my range but plenty close to Thunderfoot who stopped him in his tracks.

"Nice shooting," I said.

"Nothing to it."

We resumed walking and soon Pat took off again. This time the bunny came close to me and picked him off. It was turning out to be a pretty good day, despite the biting cold and the foot-deep snow.

We walked to the end of the long valley and then decided to go up the hill and hunt on top, and then back toward the farm. Pat picked up another track halfway up the hill but this bunny was luckier than his partners. He came out behind me and just out of Thunderfoot's range, and got into a hole. Poor Pat was beside himself trying to worry the rabbit from the hole but we finally convinced him to forget it by offering him some of Thunderfoot's lunch.

We got to the top of the hill and started through some really thick brush. Suddenly Pat began singing again. This time Thunderfoot's 20-gauge barked and the bunny was in the bag.

I was getting pretty tuckered out from the hill climbing so we decided to take a little break. We found a nice log and sat down. Thunderfoot shared the lunch he had brought with him.

"See, you always yell about me bringing food, but here you are eating most of it," he said.

"I don't yell," I said. "Sometimes I get a little perturbed when you clean out all my food, but I don't yell."

He grinned knowing my griping was all in fun...at least most of the time.

"Well, let's finish going out this ridge and then go back of the barn on that hill out there," Thunderfoot suggested. "Grandpa says there are a lot of rabbits on that hill."

It sounded like a lot of walking to me, but I decided to give it a try. We hunted the rest of the hill we were on and didn't see another bunny. Then we went back behind the barn and climbed the hill. Suddenly it was rabbit heaven. There were tracks and rabbit pellets everywhere. Poor Pat almost went crazy with so much rabbit smell in the air. The woods echoed with his howling and the shots from our shotguns rang out in the cold air. We hunted for another two hours and ended up a long, long way from the farm.

"We better start back," I said. "It's going to be dark in about half an hour."

"I want to try that one last brush pile," Thunderfoot said pointing up the hill to a large pile of limbs from a long-ago logging operation.

"Not me," I said. "I'm going to work my way down the hill. I'll meet you by the barn."

He and Pat took off up the hill. I sat for a minute or two and let my legs rest. Then I started to move down the side of the hill.

This hillside was very steep and I was trying to be very careful to keep from sliding all the way to the bottom in an uncontrolled descent. I was getting pretty winded and stopped next to a tall thin dead elm. I leaned back against the tree to rest.

As I leaned on the tree, I heard a cracking sound. Then everything was quiet.

The next thing I knew, I wasn't tired any more. I wasn't breathing hard and I was cold. It was also very dark. Suddenly I realized I didn't know for sure where I was. I sat in the snow and then I could hear my name being called from quite a long way away. I wasn't sure if I was awake or dreaming. Soon the sound got louder and I could see a light moving through the trees. "Holy cow," I thought to myself. "Maybe I'm dead."

Then the light got real bright and I could hear Thunderfoot's voice. "Hey, are you ok? Hey, can you hear me?"

I shook my head and suddenly my face got all wet. Pat was lapping my face with his large wet tongue. I realized I was sitting in the snow on the side of the hill. Thunderfoot was holding a flashlight in my face looking at me with a strange look on his face.

"Get that light out of my eyes," I said somewhat impatiently. I pushed Pat back. "Jeez, Pat needs a breath mint." I tried to stand up but my head started to throb and I got dizzy.

"What happened?" Thunderfoot asked. "I waited for an hour, and I thought you were lost, so I got grandpa's flashlight and found you sitting here in the snow."

I looked around and the top five or six feet of the elm tree that I had been leaning against was now lying in the snow on either side of me...split in two. "It looks like the top of this tree broke off when I leaned against it and hit me on the head," I said. "It must have knocked me out."

"No way!" Thunderfoot said. "That's really cool. I never saw anybody who was knocked out before."

When I struggled to my feet, everything seemed to be working but I had a terrible headache. "I guess I'm ok, let's get out of here."

We started down the hillside and soon got to the valley and then back to the farm. We thanked grandpa and loaded up the pickup for the drive home.

"Are you sure you're ok?" Thunderfoot asked.

"Yeah, I guess so."

"Then you'll be able to help clean the rabbits probably."

"I suppose I will."

"That was kind of scary. You could have been hurt real bad." He paused for a long time and then I could see his grin in the light from the dashboard. "It's a good thing you have such a hard head," he said.

Thanks, Thunderfoot.

Hail, Hail, the Gang's All Here

Spring and walleye fishing had become almost synonymous around my house. Each year, as the ice began to melt and the river began to open up, Thunderfoot and I spent a day getting the boat ready for our first spring walleye fishing trip.

One day we had the boat in the back yard and had run an extension cord to the batteries. We were puttering around, putting the gear back into the compartments.

"I didn't think we had this much stuff," Thunderfoot said as he lugged the fourth load from the storage closet to the boat. On his three previous trips he had carried rods and reels and tackle boxes. This time he was bringing the net and the toolbox that held extra spark plugs and the ever-popular roll of black tape that could fix almost anything.

"What's left in there?" I asked.

"Just the raingear and boots and life jackets," he said as he opened one of the tackle boxes and began sorting plugs and hooks and other items into piles. "It looks like somebody just threw all of this stuff in here last time and didn't put things where they're supposed to be."

"I wonder who that could have been?" I asked. No reply. Soon he had the tackle box empty, and we began putting

things back where they belonged. It took nearly half an hour, and we had three more tackle boxes left to do. Thunderfoot began working on number two while I fired up the grill and cooked half a dozen hot dogs.

"Corne and have some lunch," I said. "We can finish up when we're done eating."

I didn't have to call twice. Thunderfoot came on a run, then inhaled four of the hot dogs and the majority of a large bag of chips in just a few minutes. He washed it all down with a couple of pops.

"Ahhh. That hit the spot," he said.

"Can you tell me what you ate?" I asked, finishing my second dog.

"A hungry boy must eat," he replied, grinning.

We cleaned up the lunch plates and went back to work on the tackle boxes. In a couple of hours, we had the boat all ready to be launched the next morning.

Thunderfoot stayed over that evening, and we were up at first light, heading for the Mississippi River. We stopped for a good breakfast, and a short time later we were backing the boat into the water. I parked the truck, and after a little smoking and choking, the motor roared to life. We headed off for the darn where, hopefully, we'd meet some hungry walleyes.

The boat ride to the darn was brisk. Thunderfoot soon slid off his chair into the bottom of the boat, where he curled up like a turtle. I had to continue staring into the cold wind. Tears ran back on the side of my head as I slowed and carne to a stop near some other boats that were drifting and jigging for walleyes.

Thunderfoot crawled out of his nice warm nest and stretched. "You look cold," he said, grinning. "It's nice and warm down there out of the wind."

"If you think I'm going to let you drive the boat just so I can stay warm, think again," I said.

He shrugged. It was a nice try.

We soon joined the pack of boats jigging for walleyes. It didn't take long for Thunderfoot to jerk back and start reeling up the first fish of the day. He boated a respectable fish, then turned to show me. "This is what we're after," he said, chuckling.

The sun rose and the day turned into one that was almost too nice to be true. The temperature rose to the mid-fifties, the wind was nice and calm, and the fish were biting. We made drift after drift and caught lots of fish. Once in awhile, we put one in the live well, but most were released. The limit was six per person, and we didn't want to reach that number too soon.

By mid-day the sky had begun to cloud up, but the temperature stayed nice and the fishing was still great. I noticed that some of the other fishermen were putting on raingear, so I looked to the west. Some very ugly black clouds were coming our way. The temperature was also beginning to drop. It looked as though our dream day was going to turn on us.

"We'd better get our raingear out," I said. "It looks like we're going to get wet."

Thunderfoot reached down and opened the compartment that held the life jackets and raingear. He gave me a worried look. "It seems that I might have forgotten to put them in the boat yesterday," he said.

"What? No life jackets or raingear?"

"Well, you remember how good of a job I did on rearranging the tackle boxes? I kind of got caught up in that and forgot to go back to the closet for the last load."

"Oh, boy. What are we going to do now? We're illegal without life jackets, and we're going to get wet without raingear. "

The storm was getting close real fast. We decided to ride it out and then go to shore and buy a couple of cheap life jackets. That way we would be legal for the rest of the day.

"A little rain never hurt anybody," Thunderfoot said bravely as the first drops began to splatter into the bottom of the boat.

The little sprinkle soon became a downpour, and in a minute or two it changed to hail. In another minute, it became lots and lots of hail. We both hunkered down in the bottom of the boat as the hailstones pelted us and began filling the boat. Thankfully, they were fairly small, but they were plenty large enough to hurt real bad as they smashed into our bodies.

As quickly as it had begun, the storm was over. The bottom of the boat was about two inches deep in hailstones. Thunderfoot sat up and looked around, kind of dazed.

"Holy cow. That was pretty cool," he commented. "Yeah," I said. "That was lots of fun."

All around us, fishermen in other boats were coming back to life. However, we were the only ones who weren't in raingear, the only ones soaked to the skin.

"It's not going to take long for me to be real cold," I predicted.

"No kidding. I'm soaked, too," Thunderfoot said. He checked the live well, counting the fish we had in it.

"We're three short of a limit," he said.

We decided to try to get the last three and then head in, but before long we were both shivering and decided to call it quits. "We've got enough fish. A limit isn't that important," I said. He agreed with a shivering nod.

The ride back was torture. The wind felt like it came from a freezer now that I was wet, but we finally got there and I walked stiffly up to get the truck. Thankfully, we got the boat loaded without any of the usual first-time-of-the-year problems and pulled it up into the parking lot to stow the gear and tie it down.

"I guess this isn't so bad after all," Thunderfoot said as we worked on the boat. "We got some nice fish and had a pretty good adventure." He scooped up a few handfuls of hail and put them into the live well. "We don't even have to buy ice to keep the fish fresh." He gave me a huge grin.

Thanks, Thunderfoot.

The Best Laid Plans

Thunderfoot and I had been up for four mornings in a row. We were "turkey listening," as he liked to call it, and we thought we had everything figured out. Every morning, a group of hens came down a little draw and through a gate in the fence, then headed into the corner of a hay field to eat and preen. Half an hour later, two to five toms came down the same path and joined the hens, showing off their huge tails and strutting in front of them, hoping to impress them with their superior beauty and size.

We had been across the field each morning, watching this little parade, and tomorrow morning we were going to be waiting for the show with our gun ready. It was Thunderfoot's season. I was going along as caller, so he could concentrate on shooting. Actually, he wasn't too bad a caller himself at home, but he kind of got stage fright when we got into the woods, so he always felt better if I did the calling.

"We're going to spoil their morning tomorrow," he said, grinning at me through his head net.

"Yeah. They've been here every day, so we should be in great shape if we can get in without spooking them."

We slipped back down the hill and took off for home, feeling pretty smug.

The next morning, we snuck up to the corner of the field and put four hen decoys and one jake out just in range of the gun. Then we slipped through the fence and got into comfortable positions to await the coming dawn. I was beginning to get a bit drowsy when an owl hooted up the valley and was answered by a gobble. Thunderfoot looked over his shoulder at me and grinned. Soon we heard another gobble, followed by another and another. There were turkeys all around us.

In about twenty minutes, we saw a hen fly down off the hill and land in the field about a hundred yards from us. Then several more hens came flying down. They began feeding and going about their business, slowly moving our way toward what they thought were more hens.

Meanwhile the toms kept up their gobbling, some coming closer, some going the other way. I called every few minutes, and we soon spotted one that seemed interested in my calling. He would gobble furiously every time I called, so I began calling more urgently. He got hotter and hotter.

"He's coming right down the trail to the gate," Thunderfoot whispered. I nodded quietly.

"Turn a little to the right," I said. "Then you'll be able to shoot if he decides to go toward the real hens instead of coming to the decoys."

He nodded and very slowly and quietly slipped to the right, giving himself a wider shooting range. He did the move with almost no noise or motion, and I was impressed by how good a woodsman he had become in the past few years. He had made a lot of progress since I had dubbed him Thunderfoot.

The real hens began feeding toward us and were soon positioned just below our fakes. I looked out of the corner of my eye and saw the bluish-white head of a tom coming down the field, right alongside the fence we were sitting by.

"He's coming right by the fence, to the right," I whispered. Thunderfoot moved his head in a very slow nod and repositioned the gun a bit.

As the hens came closer, they began clucking and talking among themselves and looked up toward the tom. He stopped and displayed for them, but they seemed unimpressed and went on feeding. He stood there for a few minutes, turning from side to side so the hens could get a good look, then laid his feathers back down and started walking along the fence again.

I heard the faint click as Thunderfoot slipped the safety off and slowly moved the gun up to his cheek. The tom came closer and closer. Thunderfoot followed him with the gun until he was just a few feet away from our decoys. I had always told him that if a tom was coming toward you, you should let him come. The closer he is when you fire, the longer it takes him to run away if you miss.

I had the urge to whisper "shoot," but I figured he knew what he was doing. He held the gun on the tom, and I could see his index finger moving when I noticed that he was raising his head. Suddenly he fired. The tom stood there for about two seconds with no idea what had just happened, then ran into the field a short distance away and stood there, looking around.

"Shoot him again," I whispered loudly.

Thunderfoot was just sitting there with his mouth hanging open. He heard me and brought the gun up to shoot again, but he hadn't ejected the used shell. He had to bring it down again to eject it and feed another into the chamber. Of course, all of this commotion gave our position away to the tom, which by now was hightailing off down the field toward friendlier places.

I pulled my head net off and stuffed it into my pocket.

Thunderfoot never moved.

Finally, after several minutes, he turned around and looked at me. There was a look of utter disbelief on his face.

"He was only ten yards away," Thunderfoot said. "I can't believe it!"

I grinned. "What do you think happened?"

"Must be bad bullets."

"I think the bullets are okay. Think about it."

He pondered for a minute or so and then shook his head.

"I raised my head up to see what happened when I shot," he began. "I brought the front of the gun up and shot over him."

"Yup. I saw you raise your head," I said. "At least you know what you did wrong, so hopefully you won't do it again."

"Boy, you can be sure of that. What now?"

I looked at my watch. It was getting close to time for us to head back to town. He was allowed to miss his first class of the day, but he had to be at school by about nine.

"I guess we'll call it quits for today," 1 said. "Maybe we'll get another chance tomorrow."

We gathered our gear and picked up the decoys, leaving

everything in a pile just inside the fence, where we could find it the next morning.

I dropped Thunderfoot off at home. While he was getting ready for school, I drove to the local sporting goods store and bought a set of fiber-optic sights for the shotgun. Then I drove back to his house and picked him up.

"I bought you a little present while you were showering," I said, tossing the package to him.

"Cool! These should make me keep my head where it's supposed to be."

"They can't hurt," I said.

When we got to the school, he jumped out and started up the walk. Then he stopped and came back to the truck.

"I hope you're not mad at me for missing."

I grinned at him. "Nope. What would we do tomorrow at four o'clock if you hadn't missed? Besides, this will give me some ammo the next time you start telling stories about me."

"You won't tell anybody, will you?" Who, me?

Thanks, Thunderfoot.

Thunderfoot Speaks

Now that I've seen all the stuff Dan wrote about our times hunting and fishing together, I can hardly believe we did so much crazy stuff. But we really did.

Sometimes I think he makes things sound a little worse than what really happened, but all of the stuff he wrote about is true, and actually happened. A lot of the time, he blames me for stuff that I don't think was my fault. But you know how old guys can be.

We've done some cool stuff and had a lot of fun. But really, when you think about it, we didn't do anything out of the ordinary. It was regular outdoor stuff, but we seemed to always have fun doing it, even when it didn't turn out like we planned.

I guess we don't take things too seriously. Don't get me wrong-we try hard to catch fish and get game, but if we don't it's not the end of the world. Some of our best times fishing or hunting have been fishless or gameless, but we still had a good time trying.

One thing we both agree on all the time is that being out in nature is the best part of any trip. Coming home with lots of fish or game isn't as important as being outdoors and enjoying the cool stuff you see in a marsh or woods.

I've sure enjoyed doing all the things you've read about, and I hope you've enjoyed reading about them. It has been a good time, and I'm looking forward to lots more adventures in the future. Thanks for reading this book, and watch for us on the water or in the marsh. I'll be the one with the big grin on my face.

Your Buddy, Thunderfoot.

About the Author:

Dan Bomkamp is an avid outdoor enthusiast. He grew up along the Wisconsin River and has made his home there since his college days at UW-La Crosse. He has been involved in the sporting goods industry for many years and began his writing career by writing short stories for outdoor magazines in the early 1980s. He has hosted 30 foreign exchange students from 11 countries and has traveled to Europe to visit many of them.

His other books include: *More Adventures of Thunderfoot; Thanks Thunderfoot; Voyageur; The Gosey; Big Edna; Lost Flight; and Tag.* He lives in Muscoda, Wisconsin with his Golden Retriever, Katy. You can contact the author at:

danbomkamp@live.com,

or visit his website:

www.danbomkamp.com